"Let there be light!" said God,
  and there was light!
"Let there be blood!" says man,
  and there's a sea!

—Lord Byron, *Don Juan*

"Let them drown in their own stinking sea of blood!"

—Mack Bolan,
THE EXECUTIONER

THE EXECUTIONER: Boston Blitz

by

Don Pendleton

PINNACLE BOOKS • NEW YORK CITY

This is a work of fiction. All the characters and events portrayed in this book are fictional, and any resemblance to real people or incidents is purely coincidental.

THE EXECUTIONER: BOSTON BLITZ

An original Pinnacle Books edition, published for the first time anywhere.

ISBN: 0-523-00412-5

First printing, July 1972
Second printing, September 1972
Third printing, October 1972
Fourth printing, November 1972
Fifth printing, June 1973
Sixth printing, March 1974
Seventh printing, August 1974
Eighth printing, May 1975

Printed in the United States of America

PINNACLE BOOKS, INC.
275 Madison Avenue
New York, N.Y. 10016

To all the loyal Bolan-watchers out there who have kept the faith and given meaning to his war, this closer look into the man is gratefully dedicated.

dp

UNIFORM CRIME NETWORK—US/DOJ—ADVISORY SPECIAL****ConUS Alert

Subject
Mack Bolan, also known as "the Executioner" . . . operates also under various cover names, usually of Italian or Sicilian origin. American Caucasian, age 30, height 75 inches, weight about 200. Color of hair varies, normally dark. Eyes blue ice, penetrating, obviously highly developed night vision. Sometimes affects costume of black combat garb, commando style, but also known to wear various innocuous outfits in subtle applications of "role camouflage."

Characteristics
Considers the entire world a jungle and regards himself as final judge of who shall survive and who shall not. By conservative estimates, has slain more than 1,000 denizens of the American underworld; considers himself "at war" with all elements of the crime syndicate everywhere.

Combat veteran of Vietnam, highly skilled specialist in "destruct missions" against enemy commands; received nickname "the Executioner" in Vietnam by virtue of high proficiency this regard. Considered highly adept at penetration/intelligence techniques; military tactician and strategist of highest order; a master at both the "quiet kill" and the "massive kill" disciplines of jungle guerrilla warfare. Expert marksman, various personal weapon categories; skilled armorer and munitions man. All of foregoing constitute subject's M.O. Wages all-out warfare using all facets of the combat character. Identifies, infiltrates and destroys "the enemy"—sometimes with wiles, sometimes in full-dress frontal assaults. Has been known to use various personal combat weapons as well as field mortars, bazookas, demolition devices, etc.

Primary personal weapon, however, appears to remain a 9mm Beretta Brigadier equipped with silencer, obviously worked in for precision kills at close range. Latest personal side-arm, described as "a big silver hawgleg" by official witness has been identified as a .44 caliber autoloader, "the .44 AutoMag." This latter weapon exhibits impressive accuracy at extremely long ranges and should be considered equivalent in every respect to a big-game rifle. During latest campaign, subject was observed wearing both weapons at once.

CAUTION . . . subject is regarded as extremely quick on the draw with explosive-reaction combat instincts.

Special info

Subject is in continual "state of war" and is considered highly dangerous. All LEO urged exercise extreme caution—DO NOT ATTEMPT MAN-TO-MAN ARREST.

Subject appears to avoid police confrontation and

is not known to have ever assaulted or fired upon LEO; however subject is considered desperately defensive and in constant jeopardy via various determined underworld elements. A rumored "open contract" in amount exceeding 100-thous attracts attention of miscellaneous freelance gunmen in ever-increasing numbers. Subject is therefore under continual duress AND IS EXTREMELY DANGEROUS TO APPROACH. Various regional LEA have unofficially authorized "Extreme Precaution Apprehension"—shoot on sight, to kill.

Background info
Hometown friends, teachers, GI companions, etc. describe subject as mild-mannered, likable, well adjusted—often even as "soft hearted." Welsh-Polish extraction, eldest of three children. Mother, father, teenaged sister victims of violent death while subject serving Vietnam combat zone. Brother Johnny, age 15, sole survivor, escaped with severe gunshot wounds. Subject granted emergency furlough from Vietnam to bury family and arrange care minor brother. "Home-front war" began during this period and subject declared AWOL, subsequently military deserter. Following victory over hometown underworld elements, subject pursued successive campaigns in Los Angeles, Palm Springs, Phoenix, Miami, DC, France, England, NYC, Chicago, Las Vegas, Puerto Rico. Most recent war zone was San Francisco, where subject crushed powerful West Coast criminal conspiracy with international implications. Unofficial police sympathy noted various quarters LEA, recommend indoctrination programs emphasizing PUBLIC MENACE aspects of subject's illegal crusade.

Rumors absolutely unfounded repeat unfounded

and untrue that various federal agencies are supporting subject's private war.

Forward look
Preliminary indicators show subject headed for new confrontation in or near original battleground where brother Johnny has been in protective concealment in private school. Rumors persist that Johnny Bolan has been kidnapped and spirited away by unnamed underworld elements, probably as an attempt to lure subject into inadvantageous confrontation with "enemy."

Informant also suggests that one Valentina Querente was kidnapped with Bolan youth. Miss Querente is reportedly fiancee of subject and has also been in protective concealment.

If rumors prove true, urge all LEO in eastern U.S. gird for Executioner War without past parallel in ferocity. Similar personal situation is believed original cause of the Bolan wars. It is felt that subject will now be in furious runaway mode with all restraints abandoned.

All LEO cautions should be considered doubly emphasized.

EOM. Brognola/Justice sends.

1: The Message

At about two o'clock on a broodingly overcast Monday afternoon in Boston's North End, a tall man with peculiarly icy eyes descended upon the modest billiard parlor owned by small-time *Mafioso* Julio LaRocca.

Marty Cara, presiding over the beer bar at the front of the pool hall, was taking advantage of a business lull and preparing for the usual late-afternoon rush.

Two older citizens of the neighborhood nursed beers and talked quietly at the end of the bar.

At the rear, two pool tables were in noisy use by a party of North End youths who should have been in school.

Proprietor LaRocca, a squatly built man of about 35, was quietly pursuing a solitary game of billiards at the opposite side of the house.

Bartender Cara looked up expectantly at the entrance of the new arrival, then reacted visibly with a nervous movement toward the rear of the establishment.

The visitor wore a conservatively tailored business suit and a light topcoat, rubber-soled shoes with ripple threads, no hat. The topcoat was open in front and flapping to the sides as the man walked. He halted

Cara with a scowl and an almost imperceptible movement of the head.

The bartender jerked to a frozen stop and, in a voice with absolutely no air pushing it, inquired, "Yessir?"

The tall man issued a single, cold, command. "LaRocca."

"He, uh, what's that, sir?"

The man said it again. "LaRocca."

Cara threw a panicky glance toward the billiard section. "Back there," he whispered.

The tall man with the icy eyes said, "Let's go."

Bartender Cara reluctantly led the way, walking stiffly several paces ahead of the caller. He ignored a crack from one of the kids at the pool tables and made a careful turn into the billiard area, halting across the table from the boss.

"Guy here to see you, Mr. LaRocca," he breathlessly announced.

LaRocca deadpanned a shot off the cushions; then, without looking up from his game, replied, "So?"

"I guess you better talk to 'im."

"I don't *better* talk to nobody, Marty," the "beast of Richmond Street" reminded his employee.

"He's, uh, right here, boss."

"So I'll be with him in a minute, right here," LaRocca said.

He was lining up the next shot when a small metallic object fell to the green felt directly behind the cue ball.

LaRocca's shoulders hunched slightly. He glared at the intruding object, then something kindled deep within suddenly flaring eyes and he froze there, poised into the shot and staring at the military marksman's medal which had joined the game—and which could have but one significance.

A frigid voice above him suggested, "Finish the shot, Julio. A bucket of blood says you don't make it."

The chatter at the pool tables directly opposite abruptly ceased. A youthful voice over there gasped, "Isn't that . . . is that . . . ?"

Someone else whispered, "Shut up!"

LaRocca was still frozen by the marksman's medal. Time moved sluggishly on, and the silence became a living presence. Presently, in a heavily thickened voice, the *Mafioso* growled, "Whatta you want here with me?"

"Figure it out," the ice man suggested.

LaRocca straightened suddenly and threw the cue stick at the visitor's head, scrambling away in the same motion in a desperate run for life.

The tall man seemed prepared for the move. He swayed back in easy avoidance of the cue stick and immediately a black autoloading pistol appeared in his hand, seemingly from nowhere. It was equipped with a silencer, and it quietly coughed out two sighing little reports of death on the wing.

The first bullet plowed into LaRocca's head, just behind the ear, and the second splattered into the temple. The beast of Richmond Street hit the floor in a skid which he never felt and came to rest in a growing pool of blood which he would never miss.

Someone in the background exclaimed, "Jesus!"

Marty Cara was transfixed at the side of the billiard table, eyes glazed with horror and staring at the ugly black weapon in the killer's fist. His chin dropped and he stammered, "I'm not—honest, I'm not . . ."

The tall man commanded, "Tell them! I'm here. Tell them somebody knows why! Tell them!"

Cara's eyes remained on the weapon. He licked his lips and replied, "Yessir, I will, I'll tell them."

The icy eyes raked the witnesses at the other side of the room. Two of the boys tried smiles that failed. One carefully put down a cue stick and pointedly showed that both hands were unencumbered.

The man addressed that side of the house. "Spread the word." Then he sheathed his weapon in a rig beneath his coat and walked away from there.

Cara slumped against the table and weakly passed a hand across his face.

Several of the boys ran to the front of the building to cautiously peer through the window.

Two others haltingly approached the remains of Julio LaRocca.

"Did you *see* that fuckin' *Beretta?*" one asked in awed tones.

"Yeah, but Julio didn't," the other replied. "He never saw *nothing!*"

One of the oldsters from the bar had moved up beside Marty Cara to stare unemotionally at the interrupted last game of billiards. He reached over and picked up the marksman's medal and rubbed it between thumb and forefinger.

"That was Mack Bolan, wasn't it?" the old man asked in a quiet Italian accent.

Cara took a shuddering breath. "Yeah. The Executioner. Never saw him before, Gino, but I knew it was him the minute he stepped in here. Something—I don't know, the way he walked, the way he looked at me. I just knew."

"Wonder what he wants here."

The bartender again shuddered. "Can't you see? Hell, can't you see what he wants?"

A few minutes after the hit on the Richmond Street pool hall, an excited runner burst into the back room of a small bakery in the same neighborhood—Boston's "Little Italy" section.

This was a "numbers shop" operated by Antonio "Gags" Gaglione, lottery king of the North End. Five men were present, including two neighborhood runners, a bookkeeper, Gaglione himself, and his ever-present gunbearer, Willie "Tumbler" Pacchese.

The bookkeeper had just completed a routine math problem on a pocket calculator while the other men stood a quiet vigil above him.

As the sixth man burst into the room, the bookkeeper was announcing, "Better lay off a couple hundred on the two-eight combination, Gags. We could get burned bad on that one."

Gaglione threw a disapproving glance at the new arrival as he replied, "Yeah, okay, I'll try to spread some around Chelsea and Revere." Then he turned full attention to the disheveled man who had just lurched into the room. "Whattaya mean running in here that way?" he growled. "What ten-year-old kid is chasing you now?"

The runner had no breath to waste and he was not spending it on elaborate explanations. "Somebody just hit Julio LaRocca!" he gasped. "Marty says it was Mack Bolan!"

Gaglione turned abruptly away and hauled a cigar from his breast pocket. "What'd you say?" he muttered.

"I said—"

"Yeah yeah, shut up. What gives Marty the idea he knows Bolan from Boston beans? Julio's really dead, though?"

"God you oughta see him, I guess he's dead enough!"

A strained quietness descended and ruled the numbers shop. Tumbler Pacchese produced a snub-nosed revolver from a shoulder holster and silently inspected it.

"Put that thing away," Gaglione commanded softly. His gaze fell on the bookkeeper. "I thought Bolan was out West somewheres," he said, as though speaking only for his own benefit.

"He was tearing up Frisco just yesterday," Pacchese put in sourly. "That's a long jump—Frisco to Boston."

"Maybe he heard about airplanes," a runner snickered.

Pacchese gave the man a hard stare. "You find something funny?" he snarled.

The runner spread his hands and turned away, muttering, "So let's all have a good cry."

A seventh presence entered that back room at that precise instant and the runner found himself turning directly into a voice of coldest steel.

"Gaglione."

The single word was spat out quietly but it carried throughout the room and with absolute authority.

The numbers' king was frozen in a flat-footed stance, bull head swiveled to the sound of doom. Pacchese's gun hand was grafted to the button of his coat, fingers spread and reluctantly pointing the way to possible salvation.

The bookkeeper was staring at the big guy who was poised just inside the doorway, his fingers gripping the pocket calculator as though he were about to run a computation of life expectancies.

Nothing was moving in that room but tumbling thoughts, racing blood, and thudding hearts.

Gaglione said, "Come on in and let's talk. When did you get to town? Been laid yet?"

Even the bookkeeper knew it was a dumb try.

The tall man with the death face tossed a marksman's medal into the room. It hit the floor and slid across to rest against Gaglione's foot.

The numbers king sighed and bent down as though to pick up the medal, but as he went down he hissed to his bodyguard, "Take him!"

That which immediately followed was somewhat blurred in the memories of the surviving witnesses. One account has a gun in Bolan's hand even before he tossed the death medal into the room; another insists that the Executioner allowed Tumblers Pacchese to make the first break, then beat him to the draw.

The evidence at the scene shows only that Pacchese died of gunshot wounds of the head and heart. His gunhand was also drilled squarely through the middle, the bullet passing on through into the abdomen—this indicating that the bodyguard was not allowed to complete the draw.

Antonio Gaglione suffered a single but massive gunshot wound through the top of the skull, this official coroner's finding substantiating the eye-witness stories that the numbers boss died while bending over to pick up a marksman's medal from the floor.

Again the Executioner left the succinct message to the survivors: "Tell them I'm here. Tell them somebody knows why."

Fifteen minutes after this attack, a plumbing and heating contractor known as "Pipes" Lavallino was gunned down in his upstairs offices near North Station, in the presence of a dozen witnesses. In an almost identical pattern, a marksman's medal and a terse message was left behind.

At four o'clock that same afternoon, an emergency session was convened at Boston's City Hall. An open circuit teleconference was conducted with law-enforcement agencies in California, Florida, New York, and Washington—with the result that "advisory" delegations were immediately dispatched from those agencies for temporary duty assignments with the Boston police.

The official report, rendered by the office of the mayor at six o'clock, concluded with this paragraph:

"Consensus opinion is that Mack Bolan has shifted his operations to this area and that a full-scale Executioner war is in store for this city and suburban communities. The Greater Boston Unified Crime Prevention procedures have been activated and placed under the central coordination of Detective Inspector Kenneth J. Trantham. Program priorities to be shared by two major efforts: (1) apprehend Mack Bolan, dead or alive; (2) ascertain whereabouts of Johnny Bolan and Valentina Querente to publicly produce them alive and unharmed at the earliest possible moment."

Tell them I'm here! Tell them somebody knows why!

By early evening, all of Greater Boston knew that the Executioner was there.

Aside from the police, however, only a small handful of now desperately frightened men knew, for sure, *why* Mack Bolan had come to town.

He had come to bust that town wide open. He had come to rattle and pound and terrorize until two very dear lives were shaken from the deadly grasp of the most malevolent criminal force in existence.

He had come to rescue his kid brother and the woman he loved from a fate which even Bolan would not contemplate.

And . . . if he were too late . . . if Johnny and Val were already beyond help . . . then only God and the devil knew for sure what Mack Bolan would do to the underworld of Boston.

At that moment, not even Bolan himself could have known.

Tell them I'm here!

Tell them somebody knows why!

It was the message from a desperate war machine, in frenzy mode. It was a message of doom. It was, in every sense, the message from a tortured soul, acting out the only course of action available.

And *somebody* in Greater Boston know why.

2: Decisions

She'd been a 26-year-old maiden schoolteacher—never married "or anything"—but a damned pretty and a savvy one and Bolan was a doomed man on the run with his life's blood leaking out of him when he first placed eyes on Valentina Querente.

She had given him first-aid, shelter, then understanding and ultimately she'd given him her love. Reluctantly he had accepted it, knowing that he was doomed, knowing that he could add nothing to her life but anxiety, misery and eventually tragedy.

But Mack Bolan was no superman. He bled like other men, he fell in love like other men and he sometimes made wrong decisions like other men.

He had made a bad decision regarding Valentina Querente. She had convinced him that, from her point of view, it would be far better to have loved and lost than to never have loved at all—that pain and anxiety were every woman's price for love and fulfillment.

All this had happened during the first campaign—at Pittsfield. Bolan had not expected to live beyond that initial engagement. And, yes, there had been a strong element of selfishness in that decision to include Val in his final bloody mile on earth. A woman's love could be a wonderful and reassuring thing to a dying man. Bolan had selfishly accepted Val's love and recklessly returned it tenfold.

And then, miraculously, he had survived the hell at Pittsfield. He saw that victory as a brief reprieve, a mere stay of sentence, and he had sallied out to meet the enemy again on new ground, far away from his beloved Valentina, and he had told her at that time, "I am dead. Bury me, Val. Mourn me if you have to, but make it brief. Then pull your life together and give that bright love of yours to a guy who can give you something valuable in return, something better than a handful of ashes."

Val had not buried Mack Bolan. She had, as it were, ressurected him—via the kid brother, Johnny. Very quietly and with the connivance of sympathetic local officials she'd had herself declared Johnny Bolan's legal guardian, and she had gone with him into hiding.

"Protective concealment" for Mack Bolan's brother had been, of couse, an entirely necessary thing. Simple vengeance alone would have been motivation enough for a rub-out of the kid brother. More than vengeance, though, mob possession of Johnny's fate would give them an influence over their hated enemy which could probably never be gained via any other method.

Valentina had voluntarily cast her fate beside Johnny's. There was nothing linking her to the Bolan wars nor to Bolan himself, not until she allied herself with his only surviving relative.

So, yes, Valentina Querente was a very special item in Mack Bolan's heart.

As for Johnny Bolan—the kid had been a mere toddler when big brother Mack had first gone off to war . . . that time, in an infinity called Korea. Johnny had grown up with that soldierly image forever in front of him. Mack had written him personal letters, at least once each month, throughout those long years between toddler and teen-ager. He had sent him souvenirs and gifts from exotic lands, and he'd taken the kid camping and vacationing during those infrequent visits home.

Actually, despite the years and miles of separation between the two, these brothers probably had closer bonds of family and friendship than is usually found in a normal home environment.

Mack had forever been the hero in young Johnny's life, always larger than life, perfection personified, the "dream" big brother of every kid who'd ever grown up without one.

Upon leaving Pittsfield that final time, big brother Mack had given Johnny this parting word of advice: "Make something of yourself. Forget the past, forget me. Mom and Pop and Cindy are buried out there in Hillside Gardens. And so am I, Johnny, so am I. So you're the last Bolan. Make it count. For all our sakes, Johnny, make it count."

Johnny Bolan did not, *could not*, forget. His world had been snatched away from him by forces that he did not control and which he could not fully comprehend. Brother Mack had remained the shining symbol of strength, courage and security in a world suddenly turned hostile and unbelievable.

The kid had kept a scrapbook of the Executioner's adventures against an enemy which was also considerably larger than life, and it must have been a terrible temptation for him to confide his secret to close friends at the private academy which was sheltering him and Valentina—he as a student, she as a faculty member.

Valentina herself had been "agitating" for another meeting with the man she loved. "One hour," the contact had relayed to Bolan just very recently, "she wants one hour."

"I don't have one," was Bolan's curt reply.

What he had meant, of course, was that he would not risk their lives with the contamination of his presence. Wherever he walked, death strode along with him—and he simply would not cross their paths with his blood again, not ever.

But now, it seemed, fate or destiny or whatever moved the universe had decided to entertwine those precious lives with his once again, and Bolan had found that he had considerably more than "one hour" to offer to Valentina Querente and Johnny Bolan.

He had a lifetime to spend on them, and he would gladly spend it.

Life, after all, had boiled down to a matter of minutes or hours at best, anyway, for this doomed warrior of the damned.

"I want them alive," Bolan wrote in his journal during that tense flight from West Coast to East. "But more than I want them alive, I want them delivered from terror. I have seen too many turkeys on the Mafia's doorsteps. If I find Johnny and Val that way, I'm afraid I'll very probably lose my mind. I have to determine, first, that they are alive and well. Then I will do anything to spring them. I'll make any deal, take any action that includes rockbound guarantees of their safety. But first . . . first those bastards had better be able to show me two alive and unharmed people who never in their whole lives did anything mean or shameful. If I find two turkeys, instead . . . then God help us all."

A "turkey" is the term given to what is left of a human being after a particularly gruesome method of of torture-interrogation or sometimes mere revenge favored by certain underworld mentalities. A "turkey" is a being who is biologically alive but physically shredded and mentally reduced to a shrieking bundle of mindless nerve-endings pleading for that final mercy which is delayed to the last possible tortured, screaming moment.

And, yes, Mack Bolan had encountered one turkey too many in his wars already. He fully expected to be one himself, sooner or later.

He was, in fact, prepared to trade himself for two other likely candidates.

First, however, he had to be certain that there was something left to trade for. Two pathetic turkeys-in-hand were of absolutely no value to the Executioner . . . nor to the world at large.

So he had to do a job which several hundred cops were already finding impossible. And he was going about that task in the only way he knew. "Somebody" was playing it cozy as hell, cute as hell—or maybe just plain scared to hell. Whatever the motives, the kidnappers had left no word, no threats, no ultimatums —no clues whatever as to their intentions with regard to the kidnapped pair.

Bolan had to break that silence.

He had to learn the name of the game, and he had to learn it damned quick, before all his options were removed by the pace of events.

As a prelude to that triple-punch Monday-afternoon hit on Boston's lower-Mafia echelons, another bit of background unfolded into the Executioner's Boston Blitz.

In the early pre-dawn hours of that fateful Monday, a heavy black sedan nosed into the loading area of a public warehouse near Constitution Wharf and came to a halt near a public telephone booth.

The lone occupant disembarked and leaned casually against the side of the vehicle while lighting a cigar. He was a youngish man with dark features and a sort of devil-may-care tilt to his head. Well dressed and handsome with a quick and intelligent face, the man was Leopold Turrin and he had balanced for several years on the sharp edge of a very dangerous blade.

Turrin was a *Caporegime* of a western Massachusetts Mafia family.

He was also an undercover police officer who had infiltrated the mob through a blood relationship with a former *Capo*, and he had moved slowly but surely through the ranks to a position of trust and importance in the far-flung underworld organization.

Once, Bolan had been sworn to kill Leo Turrin. That was before he learned the deeper truth of the man. Now Turrin was Bolan's closest friend and staunchest ally. The relationship was, of course, a furtive one. It would be viewed with harsh disfavor by Mafia and police authorities alike.

After a precise five-minute wait, Turrin returned to his vehicle and sent the car into a slow crawl along the wharf. At a point about twenty yards down-range a tall figure detached itself from the shadows of the warehouse and slid into the front seat beside the driver.

Two sets of teeth flashed in brief smiles of greeting as the vehicle quickly swung into a wide circle and picked up speed along the reverse course.

Not until they were well clear of the pickup point and cruising casually along Atlantic Avenue did either man speak.

Bolan said, "You're looking great."

"Then I'm a liar," the other replied. "I feel terrible."

Bolan said, "Yeah. I know. Okay, what do you have?"

"Not nearly enough." Turrin was studying his friend's face, seen only briefly during the few personal contacts since Bolan's departure from Pittsfield so many lifetimes earlier. "Can't get used to that battle mask of yours, Sarge."

The reference was to Bolan's "new face"—received early in the wars through the surgical skills of another friend, now deceased. The plastic surgery had proved a futile tactic, except for the exigencies of the moment. Bolan's new face had quickly become as well known as the old one, and this was chiefly due to his decision to use his new look as combat camouflage rather than as retirement insurance.

Bolan said, "Don't call it a battle mask, Leo. It's a fear pack. My guts are crawling. What have you found?"

"First of all," the *Mafioso* cop replied, "the roll call on the mob side of the street keeps drawing total blanks. I can tell you this much—the snatch wasn't engineered by any of the nationals. The Talifero brothers are still in a Vegas hospital and both are still on the critical list. So the national *gestapo* is in disarray and probably will be for awhile." He showed his passenger a wry smile. "To show you how bad things really are, the *Commissione* has tapped yours truly as their man on the scene at Pittsfield. To get to the bottom of the thing, I mean. They'd never heard of Val until I started flapping my tail about the snatch. And I'm convinced that they'd had no leads on Johnny's whereabouts. So . . . from an organization standpoint, this whole thing has come as a bit of heady excitement."

Bolan's face was a study in chiseled marble—and as cold. It did not change expression as he said, "Then I guess I'm just pounding sand. I smell Boston Mob all over this thing, Leo."

"There is no Boston Mob *per se*, not anymore. But I think you're right. I don't know where you get your instincts, but . . ." Turrin smiled grimly. "I've got something from the other side of the street."

Bolan was listening.

"Your old nemesis, Lieutenant Weatherbee, thinks he's found two of the guys who figured in the snatch."

"Who are they?" Bolan growled.

"Wait, don't get up that high. These guys are beyond your reach anyway. They're in the Pittsfield morgue and—"

"Which family?"

"There's the rub. They're not connected."

Bolan groaned. "What the hell then? Freelancers?"

"That's one theory. But let me lay it out for you, and you read it for yourself."

"Okay," Bolan agreed. "Lay."

"Rudy Springer and Pete Grebchek, smalltime hoods, long records, nickel and dime stuff. Springer was released from the state prison three months ago. Grebchek escaped from Suffolk County jail, here in Boston, just two weeks ago, under rather suspicious circumstances."

Bolan said, "So?"

"So the state police found them shot to death this morning, in a car parked just off Highway 9 about five miles east of Pittsfield. Each had a bullet in the head. They'd been dead for more than 24 hours. Both of these guys have Boston addresses, Sarge."

"Keep laying," Bolan said.

"You'll like this part. A marksman's medal was lying on the seat between the two men. They'd been shot with a nine millimeter weapon, hi-shock Parabellums, same type you use. Verdict: a Beretta Brigadier."

Bolan grunted, "Cute."

Turrin said, "Yeah, isn't it? It threw Weatherbee for a minute. Just proves one thing to my mind, though. The engineer didn't know that you were starting a war on the other side of the continent at about that same time. So he must have pulled the job before the West Coast news came in."

Bolan agreed. "Okay, that figures. What else?"

"Well . . . Weatherbee has definitely placed these guys—Springer and Grebchek—or, at least, their car—in the vicinity of the academy during the period when Johnny and Val were last seen. The car is registered to Springer and several witnesses have positively identified the vehicle. It was an old beat-up Dodge with an easily recognizable backyard paint job and some very characteristic dents and crumples."

Bolan muttered, "How convenient."

"Yeah."

"And they were definitely Boston boys?"

"Yeah. Strictly small-timers. Heist men—gas stations, small markets, taxicabs, that sort of thing. No self-respecting *Mafioso* would get caught even talking to them."

"How do you read it, Leo?" Bolan asked quietly.

"They were patsies. Somebody in the mob stumbled onto Johnny and Val. I'm still trying to understand how . . . and Weatherbee is pushing his investigation along that line. Anyway, somebody stumbled onto the hide-out. For some reason, this somebody wanted a very quiet snatch. He hired the two patsies to pull the actual snatch, then he paid them on delivery with a bullet in the head. Tried to make it look like you had caught up with the guys, maybe, and rescued the kidnap victims."

"Why?"

"Hell, I don't know why."

"Okay. With that small reservation, I'll have to agree with you," Bolan said tiredly. "What else do you have?"

"That's about it," Turrin admitted regretfully. "I don't know, frankly, why our somebody is being so coy. He should be dancing a jig and thumping his chest and sending out announcements. I mean, if he's trying to smoke you into the open, he's sure going about it in a weird way."

"Maybe he wants me to sweat awhile," Bolan suggested.

Turrin grunted and said, "Could be. But this thing has all sorts of funny complications. You're not the only one sweating, Sarge."

"No?"

"*Damn* no. You understand the shape the Boston territory has been in since BoBo Binaca took the fade. Well now, look. The mob wants your head, buddy, I mean they've got a hard-on for your hide that will never go away. They want you, yeah, and they'll go to almost any fantastic lengths to get you.

But notice I said *almost*. They do *not* want your enraged hide in Boston. In the middle of the Arizona desert, maybe. Better yet, atop the highest peak of the Rockies. But not, God no, not in Boston."

"Who's the big man here, Leo? There has to be a top dog somewhere in the woodwork."

Turrin sighed. "There's another rub. Since Binaca, there hasn't been a clear line. It's been mob war, political scandals, irate citizenry, police promises, blood in the streets and just general chaos for two damn years. It stretches all around the area, even to Fall River and Providence and all points between. I guess about a hundred guys have been knocked off so far in the territorial battles. But that's been quieting down. And this is why the boys don't want a Bolan bull in their shaky little China closet. Al 88 is the *Commissione's* man here and he's been quietly putting humpty-dumpty Boston together again."

"Al who?"

Turrin shrugged his shoulders and replied, "All I've been privileged to hear is Al 88—and that's a code name, buddy, so don't sit up nights trying to match it with anything. Anyway, these people don't want your blitzing body in Boston. They feel that you'll mess up everything they've worked so hard at these past two years."

"You know what you're telling me?" Bolan commented. "You're saying the mob isn't behind the snatch."

"No, I'm not saying that. I'm saying that there is no mob in Boston. There are fragments, yeah, here and there all over the place, but they're not solidly mobbed up. The *Commissione's* guiding hand is on the scene now, though, and working diligently to get them neatly mobbed once again and part of the national picture. So—"

"So," Bolan put in, "the nationals are primarily the ones concerned about a new round of fireworks in Boston."

"Exactly. Not that the locals themselves are actively looking forward to more warfare. I mean . . ."

Bolan said, "You mean that most of them are ready to settle down and devote their energies to business as usual."

"Yeah, that's what I mean. I can't say that for all factions, of course."

Bolan said, "Okay, I'm reading."

Turrin sighed deeply. "That's about all I know for sure, Sarge. Except . . . well . . . listen, there's a Unified Crime alert out on you. The Boston cops have had enough underworld warfare, too. The citizens are edgy and the political picture is downright explosive. So . . . watch it. The first little blitz you pull, cops are going to be converging on this town from all around the country."

Bolan said, "Great. So what do you suggest I do, Leo?"

Turrin replied, "Hell, I don't know. I'm just thankful that's your decision and not mine."

"There's no decision to it," Bolan told his friend. "I'll have to play it by ear and hope for the best. But I've got to break the silence. That's for sure. I can't just sit on my tail and wait for word. It could come gift wrapped, in concrete. I can't play their game until I know what the game is. Meanwhile, there's nothing to do but to play my own game."

The undercover cop expelled a cloud of smoke, then he rolled down his window and ejected a mutilated cigar. "You know how I feel about all this, Mack. I, uh, considered myself personally responsible for those two people. I thought the security was top drawer. But it wasn't, apparently, and I guess—"

"Knock it off," Bolan softly commanded. "You know nothing is ever that tight. It just happened, that's all, and now we've got to save it. Leo . . . listen . . . thanks. I know what all this is costing you. How's the wife and kids?"

"Fine, they're fine," Turrin replied miserably.

Following a brief silence, Bolan sighed and said, "There's an angle to this thing maybe you haven't thought of. If this engineer puts the squeeze on either Johnny or Val, he'll learn anything they might be able to tell him. You and I both know that."

Turrin shivered and replied, "You could have gone all night without bringing that up. Don't think about turkeys at a time like this, Sarge."

Curtly, Bolan said, "Have to. Could they finger you, Leo?"

The *Mafioso* cop released a hissing sigh. "I guess not. I've been no more to them than a voice on a telephone, once or twice a dim face in the shadows. All they know is that I'm your friend, and theirs. Unless they've put something together on their own."

Bolan said, "Well . . . Val is pretty damned sharp. So, uh, you step very carefully, Leo."

Turrin snorted and replied, "Look who's advising who on caution."

"This three-way stretch can't go on forever, buddy. You've got to let it go, you know."

"What three-way stretch?"

"The cops, the mob, me. You know what I mean."

"You're not going to deal me out of this one, Sarge."

"Don't intend to," Bolan assured him. "But as soon as we get Johnny and Val back, then you and I have to face the reality of your situation. I could become turkey meat myself, Leo."

Turrin was giving his friend a sick look. "If that's the way you read it," he replied quietly.

"That's what I read."

"Okay. Uh, listen . . . dammit, Mack. Don't go handing yourself over to those guys. That won't help the kids any, you know that."

Bolan said, "I might be able to work something out. If it turns that way, I'd like to name you as the go-between."

"Sure," Turrin said quietly.

"Okay. What's this coming up? Charlestown bridge?"

"Yeah."

"Let me out there."

"Mack . . . dammit . . . I don't like any of this. I don't like your frame of mind. I don't like—"

"Shut up, Leo. I've had my innings. Nobody lives forever."

Turrin was glaring darkly beyond the headlamps of the car and apparently choking back some heated comment.

Bolan chuckled understandingly and said, "Cool it, buddy. We've been in worse spots. Right?"

The undercover cop growled, "Right."

The vehicle rolled to a halt on the bridge approach. Bolan gave his friend a searching gaze and asked him, "A wild guess, Leo—what is the game exactly? What do they really want?"

Turrin's eyes fell in misery from that gaze as he replied, "Same game as always, Sarge. They want you. If they can't get you whole-body, then they want to hurt you all they can. If that means sending you Val's tits and Johnny's balls in a paper sack, then that's what they'll do."

Bolan grimaced. "That goes without saying," he agreed. "But I'm not just talking about that angle. I mean, why the waiting game? Why the silence?"

The Pittsfield underboss sighed and his fingers tightened on the steering wheel. "Ever play chess, Sarge?"

Bolan replied, "The game of pawns."

"I can't see anything else, get right down to it. Considering the situation in Boston right now. Whoever snatched Johnny and Val might want something else just a little bit more than he wants Mack Bolan's head. That's why the silent game. He's trying to line something up, I'd guess. You said wild. That's about as wild as my mind can get right now."

"Maybe it's not so wild," Bolan decided. "My mind has been tracking along the same channel. Okay." He opened the door and slid quickly to the street, then leaned back inside for a final word. "Go back to Pittsfield, Leo. You'll be of better use there and I want you to stay clear of this town, at least for the rest of today. I'm hitting it, and hard. I don't want you in the way."

Turrin's face was partially masked and almost grotesque in the reflected light from the instrument panel. He said, "Johnny and Val are in the way, Sarge."

"Johnny and Val could be in South America by now," Bolan growled. "Or at the bottom of Boston harbor. Keep the ears open, Leo. We'll contact the usual way."

Turrin replied, "Yeah. Good blitzing. You know where to go, eh?"

"I know," Bolan assured him. He closed the door and faded into the night.

Turrin put the car in motion and joined the traffic to Charlestown.

Back there, he knew, went one hell of a man. One hell of a human being. And one hell of a tortured, agonized, and frustrated warrior.

The old town, Turrin was thinking, had better get set for a shaking.

She was in for an experience the likes of which hadn't been felt since . . .

Turrin's face twisted into a wry scowl.

The redcoats are coming, *hell.*

The blackcoat was already there, and he was striding angrily onto a new page of Boston history.

Turrin had seen that decision forming behind the ice-blue eyes, and there was no mistaking the meaning.

Leopold Turrin shivered.

There were times when he resented being anything other than a human being. But there were Angelina and the kids . . . he was a husband and a father. There were his duties as a cop and the patient years of painstaking undercover work that could go up in one small puff of misplaced sympathy and loyalty.

And back there, somewhere in the darkness, one hell of a unique human being was striding off into the unknown to take on the whole damned world.

Yeah . . .

There were times when Leo Turrin resented being anything other than a human being.

And he had to wonder . . . what was Mack Bolan's pet resentment? At a time of soul-wrenching decision, what did the Executioner hate the most about his situation?

The answer to that question, Turrin was certain, would be forthcoming shortly.

3: Escalation

One of the earliest recorded uses of psychological warfare occurred during the campaigns of Alexander the Great, three centuries before the Christian era. The brilliant military strategist had pushed his armies in a sweep to the borders of India when he decided to postpone further hostilities. Before withdrawing from the Indian border campsites, however, Alexander instructed his craftsmen to make a number of helmets, breastplates, horse bridles, and other items of personal armor which were many sizes too large for any ordinary man or beast. These outsized items were left behind at the abandoned campsites, and it is reported that the Indian defenders were severely demoralized upon finding this evidence of an enemy force of "giant warriors."

Mack Bolan perhaps had never heard of the psychological tactics of Alexander the Great—but it should be noted that Bolan himself habitually made full use of enemy-demoralization techniques in his own private war.

The three daylight strikes of that first probe of Boston were conducted with this specific goal in mind—to frighten and awe the enemy, to give local reinforcement to the growing legend of the Executioner's deadliness and invincibility. This, he felt, was the only practical tool in his personal campaign to free Johnny Bolan and Valentina Querente.

Bolan was a realist—but he was a soldier, not a detective. He knew that he could not hope to match the quality of actual police work being conducted on the pair's behalf. He also knew that all the odds were against the chance that routine police methods would be effective enough or quick enough to have any meaning to the end result. If not dead already, Johnny and Val were in extreme jeopardy—and their danger increased with each passing moment.

Bolan the realist knew also that the two innocents were very likely being subjected to some hellish experiences, if indeed they were still alive. He had to get to them, and he had to do it very quickly.

It was a staggering objective. Boston was New England's largest city. The city proper could probably count no more than 600 to 700 thousand citizens, but the metro area comprising Greater Boston numbered about 17 cities and towns with nearly three million people and roughly 900 square miles of real estate.

How could a man alone realistically hope to locate two carefully concealed individuals in that sprawling tangle of places and people?

The answer, of course, was that he could not possibly do so—not without an amazing bit of luck or miracle—and Bolan the realist dealt in neither such uncertain commodities.

His only chance was to try to convince the enemy that they had grabbed a tiger by the tail and to induce them to let it go, very quickly and very carefully—or else to hasten to the bargaining table without further delay.

If Leo Turrin's assessment of the Boston situation was accurate, then this could be a problem of no easy dimensions. If competitive branches of the syndicate were vying for dominance—if Johnny and Val were mere pawns in this larger struggle—then quite possibly Bolan had been lured into Boston by "somebody" who hoped to exploit the Bolan wars to personal advantage.

If this were the case, though, it seemed to Bolan that his "somebody" was playing his side of the game entirely too quietly, too cautiously, and leaving entirely too much to chance.

Bolan's foes, he knew, were realists also. If indeed the idea had been to lure the Executioner into Boston for a rampage there, then red flags should be waving all over the place. But then, too, it was entirely possible that something had gone amiss, that something had disrupted the original plan, that some last-minute foul-up had messed the play up.

There were infinite possibilities and an unlimited supply of "ifs"—and Bolan simply could not afford to wait for the logic to fall into place.

He had to make a move, and he had to do so quickly. He had to hit and keep hitting until the hurt started being felt in the right quarters.

He had begun the campaign in the most logical place—"at the border," so to speak. LaRocca, Gaglione, and Lavallino represented a triune of "Little Italy" neighborhood mobsters, unimportant in the overall weave of Mafia influence in Greater Boston, unimpressive in terms of family rank. But their executions would hardly go unnoticed, and this seemed to be the ripest spot to inaugurate the psychological war.

Bolan had not left behind in Little Italy any oversized pieces of armor, but he had left there a shadow which would grow in size with each retelling of the story—the shadow of an ice-cold hit man who strode with audacity through broad daylight and into the enemy outposts, who called out the names of his victims before coldly gunning them down, who drew and fired his weapons with such blinding speed that witnesses could not agree on details of the strikes, and who left chilling little messages to be repeated over and over again until the shock waves of those "easy hits" had spread throughout the city.

Perhaps Bolan had studied the campaigns of Alexander. Perhaps not. But the effects of his "border psychology" were just as great as that earlier warrior's.

By nightfall the entire city was quivering with the news of the Boston blitz. The newspapers had quickly seized the dramatic implications of the Bolan visit, as had radio and television newscasters—and each of the network outlets at Boston were given large spots on nationwide editions of the evening news to cover the new war in their city.

Local politicians were interviewed and quoted as "confident" that the police establishment could handle the situation. Several political hopefuls, however, recalled the two years of gangland unrest in Greater Boston and the "ineffectiveness" of the police to deal with that problem. How, they asked, could the same police hope to cope with a full-scale Bolan war?

An independent television outlet screened a hastily edited rehash of the Bolan wars from Pittsfield to San Francisco in a program which ended with a five-minute "projection" of "Bolan's Boston Blitz." The projection seemed, to many oldtimers, like an echo of the famous Orson Wells broadcast of the '30's, in which an imaginary invasion from outer space was reported.

But Mack Bolan was no Martian. He was as American as apple pie and his crusade evoked widespread feelings of sympathy and respect in this cradle-city of Americana. A local disc jockey even suggested that a "phantom ticker tape parade" be conducted along the Freedom Trail, but none took up his idea of scattering torn football pool cards and lottery tickets along the streets.

If Bolan had captured the sympathetic imagination of man-in-the-street Bostonians, though, he had also succeeded in his prime purpose; he had commanded the respectful attention of underworld Boston, and this was the name of the Bolan game.

At a "gun and hunt" club, near Stoneham in the northern suburbs, the members of that privately chartered organization got together in a hurried meeting late that Monday evening to discuss the Bolan presence in their unhappy midst.

Present at that meeting were the ruling heads of "the Middlesex Combination"—territorial bosses of northwest suburban Boston. Chief among these were Manfredo "Manny the Clock" Greco of Waltham and Terencio "Books" Figarone of Cambridge, both of whom were regarded as political and financial powerhouses in the Massachusetts crime structure.

Figarone was a legal eagle who had been disbarred from the practice of law during the Bobby Kennedy anti-crime crusade. He had also, until that time, been a visiting lecturer and honorary professor in one of the area's most prestigious schools of law.

Greco's rise to underworld eminence had come through labor circles. As a young man he had been an apprentice watchmaker in one of the nation's oldest time factories, and Manny the Clock had never lost his respect for the importance of time in human affairs. Manny was fond of pointing out that none less than Albert Einstein knew a guy couldn't amount to much unless he took time into his calculations.

Manny Greco always knew precisely what time it was—and he had called this meeting to commence at exactly ten o'clock.

At exactly ten o'clock the meeting commenced. Five territorial bosses were in attendance and they met behind closed doors in the "game room" while their cadres pondered the imponderables of sudden death over beer and peanuts in the main lounge.

The "Shot 'n Feathers" was a hardsite. Its defenses—when they "went hard"—were considered the best in the East. The location had once been a soggy marshland, bypassed and abandoned by the march of progress and even by an adjoining country club golf course, until Books Figarone stumbled onto the site and picked it up for a song some ten years earlier. Close enough to the city proper and yet isolated enough to provide the maximum privacy in a highly developed region, the site had lent itself admirably to the requirements of the Middlesex Combination and had especially proved a restful spot for jangled nerves during the past two years of gangland unrest.

A rock wall ten feet high surrounded the entire six-acre site, with the only access via a narrow wooden bridge which spanned a shallow drainage ditch across the front of the property. The clubhouse occupied a rise of ground just inside the gate. The slopes at sides and rear provided plenty of open space for skeet-shooting and rifle ranges, also a small "game yard" enclosed with chicken wire for live target shooting at trapped birds.

The clubhouse itself was not overly pretentious, consisting of a small central lounge and two elongated wings housing various recreational and business facilities. A basement room beneath one of the wings served as a pistol range with automated targets in human form which "screamed" when hit in vital spots. Beneath the opposite wing were emergency "hard rooms"—minimally outfitted sleeping facilities in tense times for overnight guests.

Behind the central lounge area was a small appendage which served as a kitchen and storehouse. The entire building was constructed of prefabricated concrete sections, and it was regarded as fireproof, bulletproof and utterly impregnable.

Even so, the ten o'clock meeting of that Monday evening got underway in an atmosphere of jittery apprehension. More than a dozen armed sentries patrolled the approaches to the hardsite and another half-dozen or so roamed the grounds inside the walls. The windows of the building, although equipped with bulletproof glass, were heavily shuttered, and armed men walked the roof.

The Middlesex Combination was taking no chances on a surprise visit from Mack the Bastard.

And, as Books Figarone angrily proclaimed at ten minutes past the hour of ten, "Look, we didn't come here to praise the guy—we came to bury him, so let's not have any more free propaganda on his behalf, eh."

"Call it propaganda if you want to," Manny the Clock shot back, "but I tell you the guy has a precision works inside his head. He's like a Swiss movement. I say he knows exactly what he's doing. If he says somebody knows why he's knocking over our downtown boys, then *somebody* sure knows *why*."

"I had a call from Al not two hours ago," Figarone argued patiently. "He assures me that they know nothing whatever about the Bolan kid. In fact, Al is more disturbed about all of this than we are."

"Speak for yourself," said Andy Nova, the boss of Medford. "I didn't even know the guy had a brother. I sure don't like the idea of bum-rapping a snatch, not with this Bolan nut picking up all the marbles. I have to go along with Manny. I think *somebody* in this town is pulling a fast one."

The lawyer from Cambridge obviously felt the situation slipping away from him. He lit a cigar and toyed with the lighter for a thoughtful moment, then he cautioned, "Look, let's not go off half-cocked. We all know what this war has cost us already. Now Al has been working miracles. We know that. Would he bring in a madman like this Bolan, at a time like this, just to tear everything apart again?"

"Maybe they already decided to write us off," Manny Greco said sourly. "Maybe they figure Boston is the least costly place to cold deck the guy. Maybe they're even doing it behind Al's back. Maybe they'd rather have Bolan than Boston. Eh?"

The Medford boss soberly nodded his head in agreement. "I been thinking pretty close to that," he declared solemnly. "I mean, just look at it. The guy has got the whole organization running scared. Everywhere. He don't care who he hits, or where. So just look at it. We ain't even in good national standing since BoBo took the powder. Why not, right? Why not maneuver this Bolan into a dead territory, get him all pissed off and hope he does something dumb, I could buy that."

Figarone was scowling with displeasure at the suggestion. He said, "We could be overlooking the most obvious answer."

"Like what?" Greco asked, leaning forward with interest.

"Well . . . what if the whole thing in a plant? I mean, what if the Bolan kid wasn't really snatched? You know?"

Manny Greco's eyes narrowed. "You mean," he replied, "what if Bolan is just inventing the snatch. Why would he do that?"

"The guy's a slicker," the lawyer said, sighing. He delicately shrugged his shoulders and added, "He's a divide and conquer guy. He works that way."

Silence descended and reigned as the troubled *Mafiosi* labored to pull together in their own heads the full ramifications of the problem confronting them.

Presently Andy Nova, the man from Medford, declared, "Well, whatever, we got to figure out something to stop the guy. I already sent my family to the island—Helen and the kids, I mean. They're staying there 'til this thing is settled."

Another boss growled an unintelligible comment which sounded like an agreement.

Silence again descended.

At fifteen minutes past the hour, Manny the Clock was glaring at his pocket watch, an impressive "railroad special" in a gold case. Someone knocked on the door to the game room. Manny returned the watch to his pocket and yelled. "Awright, it's open!"

An Andy Nova hardman pushed head and shoulders into the room and, in a tone of controlled excitement, announced, "We found something downstairs. Tramitelli thinks you should come see."

"Who come see?" Nova growled.

"All of you, boss. He says you'd all wanta see this."

The conclave of bosses exchanged a nervous round of puzzled glances, then they silently got to their feet and straggled from the room, Nova leading the procession.

The underlings in the lounge were all on their feet, hovering about in tense groups. Obviously they had already been alerted that something was up. Individual sets of eyes located respective bosses in the procession from the game room and followed their silent progress through the lounge and onto the stairway to the basement level—but neither word nor signal was passed to alleviate the tension.

The bodyguard who had summoned them pushed open the heavy door to the soundproof pistol range and stood back to allow the bosses to file past, then he entered behind them.

Hoops Tramitelli was standing woodenly in the center of the firing area, hands on his hips, staring thoughtfully at the floor. Tramitelli was Manny Greco's chief triggerman and—at any meeting of the Middlesex Combination—security chief for the entire group. A large man, heavy through chest and shoulders, veteran of many wars, the 50-year-old triggerman was also respected throughout the Boston area as an intelligent and crafty operator.

Greco called out, "What the hell, Hoops? What you been doing down here?"

"Nothing," Tramitelli replied quietly. "That's just the trouble. Nobody's been doing nothing down here."

The condition of the place seemed to be calling Hoops a liar. Private pistol cases in the weapons-storage racks had been broken open and the handguns scattered along the firing line. Ammunition boxes were smashed, their contents carelessly dumped in piles all about the place. The three automated targets were in operation and moving smoothly along their programmed paths in the target pits.

Andy Nova angrily cried, "Who the hell did this? What nut . . . ?"

The other bosses were strolling woodenly about, tentatively kicking at ammo piles on the floor and avoiding the more heavily littered areas.

Tramitelli was explaining, "I just come down here a few minutes ago, just a security check. I found it like this. Nobody else had been down here. The lock was still on the door. But this is just the way I found it."

Books Figarone quietly asked, "Who's the head cock out here this month, Hoops?"

"Charlie Sandini. I already sent for him."

A skinny youth with nervous eyes entered the pistol range and came to a frozen halt just inside the doorway, his eyes flaring.

In a choking voice he exclaimed, "Well Jesus! What's been going on here?"

"That's what we wanted you to tell us, Charlie," Tramitelli advised the duty steward.

"God I—this is the first I—God I don't know nothing about this, Mr. Tramitelli!" the man insisted.

"You're the head cock, you damn sure better know," Manny Greco declared coldly.

"I didn't even open up down here," Sandini protested. "You said just a business conference, just booze and snacks, and that's all I got ready for. I didn't even come down here all day. I didn't even . . ." The worried eyes swiveled toward Books Figarone. "That guy!" he cried.

"What guy?" the lawyer growled.

"That guy you sent out here this afternoon!"

"I sent nobody out here, Charlie," Figarone said.

"Yessir you did—remember the guy from the gun factory?"

Figarone said, "You been smoking marijuana again, Charlie. I told you to—"

"Wait a minute," Manny Greco put in angrily. "When was this, Charlie, this guy from the gun factory?"

"About five-thirty, six o'clock I think," Sandini replied quickly, gratefully riveting his attention to the other boss.

"Well what was it, either five-thirty or six, what was it?" the clockmaker wanted to know.

"God I don't know exactly, I was—wait, it was before the six o'clock news. Yeah. The guy stood there at the bar and watched the news with me for a minute before he took off. Wanted to see how the Patriots were doing. So . . . he was here altogether about a half an hour, maybe less. I guess."

The bosses had formed a semi-circle about the jittery steward. Tramitelli was standing off the side a little, staring down the range toward the whirring targets.

Figarone was saying, in that quiet purr of his, "You mean you let a perfect stranger just walk into our club, Charlie? You let him just come in here and look around and do whatever he wants to do? You didn't even come downstairs with him?"

"God, he had your card, Mr. Figarone. He said you wanted him to do some work on the pistol range. He showed me his stuff, he was from this gun factory. It all looked on the level to me. But why would he come in here and tear everything up? I mean, what is the guy, some kind of nut?"

Tramitelli was still staring at the moving targets. His voice overrode a comment from one of the lesser bosses as he said, "This nut of yours, Charlie. What'd he look like?"

"Just a guy. Wore coveralls, you know, like these service guys wear. Carried this tool kit."

"What'd he *look* like, Charlie?"

"Uh, big guy. You know, tall. Kinda young, I guess. Yeah, no more'n about thirty. Laughed a lot. You know, joking, carrying on a lot. Okay guy, I thought. You know. Lotta fun. We, uh, I even set him up a beer. God, now that's thanks for you, the guy comes down here and leaves a mess like *this*."

Tramitelli sighed loudly and sadly. "Where were the other boys while you were setting up beers?" he asked.

"Uh, well there was just Paul and Lacey. You know. We were soft until—I mean, we didn't go on alert until Mr. Greco called, about seven o'clock. We were eating supper when this guy got here."

Tramitelli again sighed and walked off toward the target pits. Greco followed a few steps behind him. Figarone was arguing loudly with the hapless steward and the lesser bosses were standing by in a strained silence.

Andy Nova pulled loose from that group and trailed after Tramitelli and Greco.

The chief triggerman reached the pits first and stood there with hands on hips and watched the automated figures go through their motions.

Nova and Greco pulled up beside him, and Nova softly exclaimed, "Well, do you see what I see!"

Tramitelli growled, "Yeah. I thought I saw it all the way from the firing line." As one of the target figures moved past, he reached out to snare an object which was dangling over the target heart.

Greco silently leaned forward and snatched another, then Nova picked off the third one.

Each object was an identical military marksman's

medal, drilled cleanly through center with a neatly punched bullet hole.

Tramitelli remained in the pits, thoughtfully tossing the mutilated medal into the air and catching it, while the other two returned to the firing line.

Greco turned his souvenir over to Books Figarone and said, "Well, there you go."

The Cambridge lawyer's facial lines settled into a deadpan expression. He said, "Let's get out of here."

The other bosses were quietly examining Andy Nova's medal.

No explanation was necessary, and apparently none could think of a fitting comment.

Tramitelli came up from the pit area and solemnly declared, "I think you'd all better beat it, Mr. Greco. The guy could've planted bombs, anything."

Greco's eyes were worried, almost panicky. He nodded and quietly commanded, "We go out in hard convoy, Hoops. See to it."

The triggerman grunted and hurried out.

The others quickly followed him up the stairs, and the lawyer from Cambridge was heard to remark, "Don't take it so hard, Charlie. You're not the first to fall for a Bolan stunt."

"He was such a straight Joe, Mr. Figarone," the duty steward was insisting. "I just don't think it could've been *him*. I mean this guy was . . . well he was an *okay guy*, know what I mean?"

And at that very moment, the "okay guy" was less than 200 yards away, patiently waiting for the Middlesex Combination to quit their "impregnable" hardsite.

He was attired for night combat, and he was no more than a softly breathing black shadow of death on a landscape carefully made ready for war.

In a snap-out rig beneath his left arm rode the

silent black Beretta. A big silver automatic, the .44 AutoMag, was worn in a flap holster at his right hip. The same weapons belt which supported the AutoMag also provided berths for a number of personal munitions. At his right knee stood an unimpressive little artillery piece which thousands of ex-GI's would recognize as a field mortar; beside it was a neat stack of 40mm mortar rounds.

The peace and quiet, out there on that no-man's-land, was but a deceptive lull before the storm which would soon engulf all of Boston in a savage sea of blood.

His time was at hand, and the Executioner was ready for the first pitched battle of the most important war of his life.

This one is for love, he told himself.

And let those others sink into their own stinking sea.

4: The Middlesex Strike

Charlie Sandini and his small garrison force remained behind, inside the Shot'n Feathers, while the other hardmen assembled in the vehicle area, under the direction of Hoops Tramitelli, forming the motor convoy.

The "point" vehicle—an eight-passenger limousine carrying nothing but granite-faced gunners—was a typical crew wagon, glossy black and gleaming with chrome. This car went on to the gate and idled there while the other vehicles formed a line at the canopy outside the lodge to pick up the VIP passengers.

Manny Greco was the first boss to appear, sandwiched between his two lieutenants and hurrying into the rear seat of a white Cadillac. One of his personal bodyguards slid into the front beside the wheelman, and another hopped into the jumpseat and swiveled about at a right angle to the three men behind him.

Books Figarone was the next man out, but his vehicle had somehow fallen into line closer to the rear; he hung back into the shadows with his bodyguards and quietly watched the operation, as one by one the Middlesex Combination exited from the club when the big vehicles inched forward to receive them.

Figarone's car appeared then—the last slot ahead of the two rearguard crew wagons. He paused beside

Tramitelli for a brief conference, then he slid inside his vehicle and made himself small behind the human barricades surrounding him.

Tramitelli was the last man on the ground. He climbed into the tail vehicle, another gleaming Continental with six gunners already inside, and contacted the point vehicle by radio.

"We go," he announced tensely. "Keep it slow and easy until I'm across the bridge, then open 'er up."

"Okay," came the reply from the head of the procession. "How about the boys out on the road?"

"I already told them. They stay until we're clear. Then they go inside and help Sandini shake the joint down."

"Right, here we go."

The gate swung open in response to an electronic command from the point vehicle and the ten-car caravan moved smoothly forward.

Tramitelli's crew wagon was swinging into the turn to the gate. The worried triggerman was sighting along the lineup of vehicles and breathing a sigh of relief when the leading car reached the narrow wooden bridge just outside the walls. The convoy was about halfway through the gate and there had been no show of hostility from the darkness out there.

He touched the mike button and told the point car, "Slow'n easy now, let's don't get too strung out."

"Okay, we—"

Those were the last words to be uttered into the synthetic peace of that war zone. A brilliant flash-up there at the point of the procession was followed by an earth-shaking explosion. The wooden bridge and the point vehicle were momentarily haloed in a wreath of fire, then bridge and vehicle fell into the drainage ditch and a fireball whoofed into the sky as a secondary explosion shattered the car, sending pieces of it raining back along the convoy.

Tramitelli's wheelman gasped, "What . . . ?"

The chief triggerman yelled, "He blew the bridge! Out! Everybody outta the car!"

Even as he spoke—and before any reaction could occur—the vehicle which at that moment was occupying the open gateway erupted into a smaller explosion and swiveled to a quivering halt, sealing the only opening in the ten-foot wall surrounding the joint.

The delayed reaction began then, with men scrambling from the vehicles all along the line, voices raised in confused alarm. From somewhere in the din were issuing bloodcurdling screams—probably from one of the wrecked vehicles.

Tramitelli hit the drive beside his car and sprinted forward along the stalled convoy, shouting angry commands. "Outta the cars! Take cover! Get the bosses back inside!"

Then a walking line of explosions descended, traveling the shoestring pattern of the assembled vehicles, unerringly on target, car-by-car transforming the gleaming convoy to smoking heaps of shattered metal and glass.

A chain reaction of fires was already erupting, fed by flaming streams of gasoline.

Guys were running around crazily like ants in a burning mound, their senses stunned by the rapidity of the attack and the shattering series of explosions.

Someone screamed, *"That's a mortar attack!"*

Tramitelli had flung himself clear of the target zone and was on hands and knees beside the wall. It was like a battlefield out there, with balls of fire erupting and smoke clouds forming and drifting skyward.

The security chief threw back his head and screamed, "Jess—Jess Accoura!"

"Yeah, boss," came a shaken reply from somewhere in the confusion.

"Take your crew outside! The guy's out there somewhere! Go smoke him out!"

It was a command which neither Accoura nor anyone else present was taking too seriously.

A voice which Tramitelli recognized as belonging to his boss, Manny Greco, screamed, "Hoops! I'm hit, I'm hurt!"

That was too damned bad, Hoops was thinking. Manny the Clock was out there in no-man's-land, outside the wall. Three other bosses were out there also—and if they were smart, they'd be a lot quieter about it than Manny was being.

Tramitelli was the war department now, and he came to a quick command decision. "Forget that, Jessie!" he yelled. "Don't nobody go out there! Everybody inside, into the joint! Come on, come on, everybody take cover inside!"

Hoops himself was already halfway there.

There was everything to lose and nothing—absolutely nothing—to gain out there in that darkness with Bolan on the blitz.

And obviously, there was little to be gained inside, either. Tramitelli was less than ten paces removed from the sanctuary of the front door when the whole joint seemed to lift itself and move away from him. Flames and thunder rose up beneath it to pummel the night, and suddenly there was no "inside" anywhere.

It was just Bolan now, leaping flames in a crazy night and a civilian army in full rout.

Indeed, "the guy could have planted bombs, or anything." And he had.

It had been a gamble worth taking, and now Bolan was thanking the universe or whatever supplied combat instincts for directing him to that Middlesex hardsite. There had been no assurance that the northwest mob would congregate there on this night of nights . . . but the instincts had suggested: *Go to Middlesex*—and the Executioner had gone.

Cracking the security of the joint had been far easier than he had been led to expect—and again the timing had been the all-important factor. He'd slipped in ahead of their hard forces, and the accommodating steward had given him more than enough unsupervised time to plant the demolition charges and to set up the spook show.

He could have blown the joint at any time, then. The radio detonators were effective over a long line-of-sight range; he could have returned hours or months later and detonated the explosives while cruising the neighborhood in his car.

He had elected, though, to ride his hunch all the way, so he'd placed another demolition device beneath the access bridge, run his mortar range fixes before darkness came.

The rest of the party had been up to the Middlesex Combination and they had not disappointed him.

He'd watched them arrive and deploy the security forces. He had marked and categorized each of these hardmen in his mental mugfile and then he'd moved quietly against them. Even before the bosses inside had all sat down with their urgent business, the Executioner had stealthily swept that blackened landscape beyond the walls, and one-by-one he'd deprived the Shot'n Feathers of its outer security line.

By the time the council of bosses were grimly filing along the stairway to "come and see" the Executioner's calling card in the basement, Bolan was in full command of the terrain outside the walls—and he had also appropriated a small walky-talky from the dead corporal of that outside guard.

Bolan could, of course, have simply blown up the hardsite while all were inside, with as good results and with far less personal hazard. It simply was not the Executioner's way, though, for he preferred to take them in open combat.

So he had watched and waited. When Tramitelli radioed the word that they were coming out, it was Bolan himself who acknowledged receipt of the information, and who assured the security chief, "It's quiet out here, don't worry."

He watched the convoy forming at the gate and deduced the departing strategv as he final-checked the range settings for the field mortar.

The nice feature of a mortar was that there was no ballistics trajectory, as in standard artillery pieces. The little shells were lobbed, not zipped in, and he could lay them inside those walls wherever he wished. Also there was no tell-tale flame or report with the firing, there were no empty shell cases or breeches to fool with—you simply dropped in the round and the whole thing flew.

A guy who knew his way with a field mortar could lay down a hell of an impressive barrage, and there was enough explosive charge in a single round to scatter an entire squad of infantry.

Bolan had figured them to come out in a convoy line-up, which meant no more than a car length of separation between each vehicle, and he'd figured to blow the bridge with the point vehicle aboard. The mortar was zeroed-in on the gate and the first round should catch one of the vehicles near enough to that opening to plug it thoroughly.

The Executioner should then have them all precisely where he wanted them—separated, confused, and as soft as a hard convoy could get.

Next he would take away their damned hardsite, then he would take away everything they could hide behind or beneath, and then by God he would put in a personal appearance and let them see what they'd bought when they snatched Johnny and Val.

The strike had gone off without a hitch. They had performed precisely as Bolan had hoped, and his little pocket detonator had done its bit with the bridge.

He watched that point vehicle wallow into the ditch and enfold itself in the Executioner's baptismal flames, then he dropped in the first mortar round and sent an exclamation point hurtling into the vehicle at the gate.

For the next 30 seconds, Bolan was too busy with the mortar to take much note of what was happening down there; he had to reset the range and reload the belching tube with each round, and he had to get off a round every three or four seconds if the assault was to fully jell.

It was not until the final mortar round had been fired that he paused for an evaluation, and what he saw would have made an artillery unit proud.

Then he switched the pocket detonator into the primary charge, pushed the button, and that was the end of Shot'n Feathers.

It was sheer panic down there when the blitzing black shadow snatched up his chattergun and loped down the road to close on the enemy.

It was mop-up time at Mafiaville, and the Executioner did not wish to deprive them of his presence for a single unnecessary moment.

He crossed the dry ditch without a pause and made his first call at the second vehicle in the line.

A mortar round had obviously dropped right through the windshield and the interior had taken the full shock of the blast. All the window glass was blown out, front and back, and the two guys up front had come apart in grisly ways.

The car was burning, a tumble of bodies in the rear was flaming with the unmistakable aroma of cooking flesh.

A rear door was sprung open, and a guy was lying half in and half out. His legs were on fire and he was still alive and struggling. The eyes were open and the guy was holding a pocket watch in his hand.

Bolan stepped forward, placed the muzzle of the stuttergun against the dying man's forehead and he immediately recognized Manny the Clock. The boss of Waltham probably did not know himself, though, at that point. Massive shock had insulated him from pain and from rational thought.

Or so it seemed. "What . . . what time is it?" Greco asked the Executioner.

"Time to die, Manny," Bolan quietly replied as he pulled the trigger, mercifully stopping Manny's clock forever.

Then Bolan went on along the line, moving swiftly through the flaming pandemonium, pausing occasionally to tickle the trigger of the automatic weapon and tidy up a loose end here and there.

The strike was less than a minute old when he reached the wall. The gateway was impassable, totally blocked by the flaming vehicle.

Bolan hesitated but a moment, then he pivoted and

ran along the rock wall, seeking the best spot to go up and over.

This one had to be clean.

For Johnny and Val, it had to be a total rub-out.

5: Hell Ground

The scene inside those walls was straight out of *War and Peace*—with all the peace removed. And it was all too familiar to the man who had brought it here. Leaping flames—strewn rubble—demolished vehicles—dying groans of the mortally wounded—stunned survivors stumbling about through drifting smoke—unmoving lumps of flesh, and the smell of blood and powder everywhere—now and then a solitary figure moving furtively into the protective darkness of the rear.

Yeah, all too familiar. Bolan threw off a tremor of revulsion—for himself, for the world he had adopted—then he steeled himself and dropped into the reality of War Everlasting.

He was instantly spotted and a distant voice screamed, "Hey, it's *him*."

A volley of fire immediately swept toward him from the darkness off to his right.

Bolan dropped to one knee, came around with the chattergun in hard argument and sweeping for effect. Someone out there screamed, then another, and the enemy fire dropped away except for sporadic and scattered reports. The gunners were out of effective range for most handguns and no one seemed inclined to shorten the distance.

Then another voice rang out from the darkness, a harshly commanding and authoritative sound. "Hank! Georgie! What the hell are you waiting for?"

Bolan was feeding a fresh clip to his weapon when Hank and Georgie apparently joined the war. Two wide spaced muzzle flashes began laying in a methodical fire on his position, and these were not going so wild. The guys had rifles, and under more settling conditions they would probably have been pretty fair marksmen. Many a fair-weather target marksman, though, finds his aim falling apart under combat conditions, and these two were destined to discover that truth the hard way.

Bolan did not give them time to settle into their mark; he came out of his drop in a running charge, the chattergun spewing from the hip and probing the darkness surrounding those rifle flashes. One of them went to hell almost instantly, the passage signaled by a gurgling scream—and the other must have lost all heart for the fight.

Silence descended, to be broken by that voice of command out there. "Come back here! Where the hell you guys think you're going? Get back—!"

Bolan threw a probing burst toward the sound, and quiet again prevailed.

After a moment another strained voice called out, "Did he get you, Hoops? Hoops? You okay?"

Bolan was moving on, moving more slowly now in a careful crouch. Again the stuttergun spoke, in a searching death pattern for those voices out there. A muffled yelp rewarded the effort, and now he could hear feet pounding the turf.

The harsh voice of command he'd heard earlier called out, from considerably farther away, "Okay, Bolan, it's your round this time. But we'll meet again."

Bolan growled, "Bet on it," under his breath, as he spun about to quit that sector and to move on to ruins in the area where the lodge had been.

There was not much left of Shot'n Feathers. Two walls remained standing—the rest was rubble with flames licking up here and there. It had been a good, clean demolition job, with the charges placed for maximum effect—a job which Boom-Boom Hoffower of the now-extinct death squad would have been proud to see.

Bolan proceeded carefully along the macadam drive, feeling his way through drifting palls of smoke, and again he came under fire. Fingers of flame were reaching for him from the earth directly ahead, accompanied by the barking of a small-caliber revolver. Angry sizzlers sang by in close passage.

The fire was coming from a guy who was lying on his back, not ten paces ahead, and he could hardly hold the gun up, even using both hands. Bolan moved unhesitatingly forward until he was standing over the guy. He kicked the gun away and said, "Nice try, slick."

The guy moaned, "I ain't got your brother. Leave me alone."

The *Mafioso* also did not have much time left for this world. Both legs were smashed and skewed out at crazy angles from the body, and blood was soaking into the clothing at his waist.

Bolan did not leave Andy Nova alone.

He left him with a mercy round in the forehead then he went on across the hellfield.

Here and there among the rubble he found a living one, dispatched him and moved on until there was nothing left for him there.

A body count would have been time consuming and

meaningless, so Bolan had no way of knowing how many had escaped to the rear—and he did not particularly care. He had brought his message, left it there for all to see and now it was time to withdraw. The sounds of warfare would not go forever without investigation; soon the cops would be pouring in, so it was time for the Executioner to be bowing out.

The wreckage in the gateway had about burned itself out. He went out past it and walked quickly up the line of gutted vehicles. Behind him, Shot'n Feathers was finding new fuel for her flames, and secondary fires were beginning to belch skyward, lighting up that forward terrain with dancing shadows.

Halfway to his own vehicle Bolan spotted a different kind of shadow on the roadway ahead, moving away from him, and this one was behaving like a drunken man—stumbling, reeling, falling only to get up and try it again.

Somebody was in a hell of a sweat to quit the hellfields. For a brief moment Bolan debated the fate of that frenzied escapee—then he sighed and stopped the guy with a line of zinging slugs across his path. The man wheeled around and turned crazed eyes upon his pursuer, then he moaned and sank to the ground.

He was a smoothie, about 50 or 55, with distinguishing silver hair at the temples and wearing an expensively tailored suit which was now a dead loss. Blood was seeping from a scratch above one eye and the face was smeared with it—but even through all the dishevelment, the Executioner's mental mugfile provided the make on Books Figarone, the law professor turned Mafia bigshot.

Bolan quietly informed him, "You're running in the

wrong direction, Professor. Cambridge is the other way."

The guy was fighting for breath—and apparently the legal-trained mind was fighting for a way to go on living. "Mack Bolan!" he gasped. "So you're the one who saved me!"

Bolan almost felt like laughing, but not quite. He said, "I saved you, eh?"

"Of course you saved me. That's a Mafia joint back there. They were holding me prisoner. They were going to kill me."

Bolan said, "Do tell"—and shoved the muzzle of the stuttergun into the guy's heaving gut.

"Wait, Bolan, wait!" Figarone cried. "God, I can help you, man! I can help you!"

Bolan told him, quietly, "That's what I'm here for, Books."

"Then you've come to the right man!" the lawyer burbled.

"You know what I'm looking for."

"Yes! Yes, I do know!"

"You know where I can find them?"

"Maybe! I'd like to try, Bolan. Let me try!"

"Then maybe you've got some life left in you," Bolan coldly advised him. "On your feet, move, let's go."

Figarone surged to his feet, he moved, and they went.

Not another word was spoken until Bolan's vehicle was reached, and by this time the Cambridge lawyer was getting his head together again.

He asked Bolan, "Where are we going?"

"To hell," the Executioner assured him. "Unless you really can help me."

The anxious man shivered and sent a final look along

the backtrail. He had just come from hell, the look seemed to say. He sighed and told his captor, "You can depend on me, Bolan. I hope I can depend on you."

Bolan did not reply, but the Mafia boss did not need a verbal response. He knew damned well that he could depend on this icy-eyed warrior to *live* in hell until his mission was accomplished. He carried hell around with him—and now, it seemed, he was carrying Books Figarone around with him.

The distant wail of sirens edged into the atmosphere.

Bolan sent his vehicle in the opposite direction.

Figarone crowded the door, maintaining as much distance as possible from that apparition of doom behind the wheel.

Yes. The guy carried hell around with him. Figarone knew. He had been there. Pretty soon, without the intervention of some miracle, all of Boston would be there.

The boss from Cambridge shivered and closed his eyes.

Yes. The guy was everything they'd said he was. And the ex-professor of law was wondering what sort of fool had decided to wave a red flag at this formidable warrior. Of all the stupid . . .

He *would* help him. By God, yes. At that moment, Figarone figured that he was as anxious to catch the fool as was Bolan himself.

But that was a miscalculation of the legal mind.

No one, but *no* one, wanted "the fool" as fiercely and as determinedly as did the Executioner.

Shot'n Feathers was but a prelude, a muted statement of that determination.

The hellfire trail had only just begun.

6: Post Mortem

A number of county cars and several emergency rescue units were on the scene when Inspector Trantham's vehicle pulled to a halt on the road outside the Mafia country club.

The Boston cop was coordinating the Greater Boston police effort during the current law-enforcement emergency and he had elected to personally respond when the first alert came down. He had heard a lot and read a lot about this angry young man they called the Executioner, and he wanted a first-hand familiarity with Bolan's handiwork.

Kenneth Trantham was 47 years old. He'd been a cop since the age of 22, which gave him 25 years on the job. He'd seen a lot of hard ones come and go, and he'd seen some sensational crimes during a quarter-century with the Boston police. But he had never met a criminal—small or large—who'd shown any real stature as a human being. They were all punks, in the inspector's judgment—scared punks who had turned to crime because they hadn't the guts to make it any other way.

And Ken Trantham knew a thing or two about scared punks. He'd grown up on the city's south side, or "Southie," where neighborhood street gangs had served as finishing schools for the restless young products of those southside streets. Back in those days a kid had to join a gang just to survive—not financially but physically.

Yeah, and Trantham knew a thing or two about street punks. He'd been one himself—but he'd had the common sense and human stature to grow beyond that sort of thing, and he'd left it 25 years to the rear. For those who had not—well, the inspector knew about those also. The more scared they got, the more vicious they became—show Ken Trantham a vicious man and he'd show you a guy who lived with curling guts.

But some cold animal thing was chewing at the inspector's own guts as he walked into that hellish scene in Middlesex County. A phantom—or an echo or something—of the old terrors was lurking there in that atmosphere of doom which was enveloping those bloodied grounds. And that phantom was trying its best to insinuate itself back inside Kenneth Trantham's guts.

He shook off the feeling of hopelessness and edged past the demolished vehicle in the gateway, then he quickly collared a uniformed Middlesex deputy, to whom he identified himself, issuing crisp instructions. "Clear that gateway," he commanded. "And get some floodlamp units in here. Get some pictures of that vehicle before you move it, though."

The deputy touched the bill of his cap and hurried away.

The two men who had accompanied Trantham to the scene straggled up behind him and stood in quiet surveillance of the devastated battle site. Both had arrived in Boston a short while earlier—one from Florida, the other from California. They were Captain Tim Braddock of the Los Angeles police and Bob

Wilson, a homicide lieutenant from Miami. Both men were veterans of the Bolan wars and had journeyed to Boston in response to the UCN alert in that area.

Trantham threw his "advisers" a troubled glance and asked, "You ever see anything like this?"

Braddock nodded his head in the quiet reply, "Yes, I'm afraid I have."

"It's a typical Bolan hit," the man from Miami agreed.

"So it hasn't been an exaggerated reputation," Trantham said.

"Some things are beyond exaggeration," Braddock replied.

The three officers trudged about the grounds for several minutes without further comment, poking into the physical evidence without disturbing it and finally the Boston cop declared, "Well . . . I can't believe that all of this is the work of a single man. I can't accept that."

"You might as well," the Captain from L.A. replied. "The guy is a one-man army, Trantham. I've been a Bolan watcher from close to the beginning. My town was number two on the guy's hit parade. Take my word for it . . . he's a phenomenon. How he's stayed alive this long is the greatest mystery. Hell, he just booms in and runs wild, with no regard for odds or whatever. He makes his own odds."

"Like a comic-strip character, eh?" Trantham observed wryly.

"Not at all," was Braddock's curt reply. "Nothing comical about Mack Bolan, believe it."

Bob Wilson had detached himself from the other two. He was standing just off the macadam drive, at a point where it curved away from the lodge and beelined toward the gate.

Trantham moved up beside the man from Miami and asked him, "How do you read it, Lieutenant? How did he manage to get bombs into all these vehicles?"

"Not bombs," Wilson thoughtfully replied. "When this place has been scraped clean and all the evidence reviewed, I'm betting you'll find shell fragments—shrapnel—imbedded in the vehicle bodies, and in many of the corpses. You'll notice also that there's no blow-out of the roadway beneath the vehicles, as you'd find with dynamite bombs. No . . . I'm betting your diagnosis will be an artillery attack. A field mortar, probably."

Braddock growled, "Yeah, the guy's no bomber. He's a hellfire guy. He probably stood out there in the open somewhere and just lobbed this stuff in on these guys—probably had them running hell-for-breakfast all over the place."

Trantham's face twitched. He said, "You could almost admire . . ."

The visiting policemen exchanged arched glances. Braddock said, "Sure, the guy's a heroic figure, you have to give him that." The big cop sniffed and added, "Hell, he saved my life once. I'll never forget that. But none of that alters the fact that he's a public menace. He's got to be stopped, one way or another."

"He's going to get stopped in Boston," Trantham replied grimly, his lips barely moving.

A plainclothes cop from the sheriff's department approached the group, walking up quickly from the back side of the property. He was carrying a flashlight and his face was twisted into somber lines. He recognized Trantham and went directly to him.

"Glad you're here, Inspector," he said quietly. "This place is a regular battlefield. Dead men are scattered all around. So far I've counted 22, and that's only a beginning."

As quietly, the inspector asked, "Recognize any of them?"

"Just about all of them," the sheriff's detective replied. "It's the Middlesex Combination, or a large part of them. Looks like he caught them bunched up in here and just laid all over them."

Trantham grunted, "Yeah. We were just looking at the mess in these vehicles."

"We'll have to rely on fingerprint identification for most of those," the detective pointed out, needlessly.

The inspector said, "Yeah, if we can get even that. Uh . . . Harley . . . do you know these men? This is Captain Braddock, LAPD—Lieutenant Wilson, Miami Metro. Detective Harley Langston, Middlesex County."

The officers acknowledged the introductions and shook hands, then Trantham told Langston, "I told one of your uniformed boys to get the light units in here. You want to see how they're doing on that?"

The sheriff's man nodded agreement, but he paused to direct a question to the man from LAPD. "You the captain who was in charge of the Bolan hunt out there?" he asked.

Braddock sighed and replied, "Hell, Harley, don't remind me of that."

Trantham put in, "Braddock's detail came closer to nailing Bolan than anyone ever has."

Langston nodded as though he were well aware of that piece of information. His eyes had remained steady on Braddock's. "I've got a book crammed full of Bolan," he said soberly. "I went over to Pittsfield after his vendetta on Sergio Frenchi, and I worked up a reconstruction of his entire routine. Later, when he was laying into your town, I thought I could work him into some sort of M.O. but hell the guy never seemed to follow any set pattern."

"That's one of the problems," Braddock admitted.

"Well I've been following his campaigns like a fan. I think maybe I've got him snockered now. I think I know what his pattern will be in this area. I'd like to talk to you about it, sort of dry-run my ideas, get your thinking on it."

Braddock murmured, "Be glad to, Harley. Any time."

"Include me in on that," the Boston cop commanded.

"I'll do that. Don't go away. Back in a minute."

The sheriff's detective strode away on his errand and Bob Wilson commented, "Patterns are one thing. Snockering Mack Bolan is quite a different matter."

Braddock growled his agreement with the idea.

Inspector Trantham said, "You gentlemen are here to advise us, not to discourage us."

"I'm here to get Mack Bolan," Braddock softly declared.

Wilson echoed the sentiment, adding, "The guy has become a national embarrassment. In fact, a national police disgrace."

"The disgrace is going to end, right here in Boston," Trantham declared. "Bolan is one of our own, you know . . . or very close to it. We know how to deal with the Mack Bolans."

Braddock and Wilson exchanged wry smiles.

They'd heard the same idea expressed before, in various places. But Mack Bolan was still loose and blitzing. And the guy never seem to tire. He seemed, in fact, to get stronger and cagier with each new campaign. And, Tim Braddock was thinking, if that last bit of logic held true, then the old town of Boston was in for a hell of a big dose of Mack Bolan before this one was ended.

Braddock knew. He'd been around Bolan's horn. And deep down, the big cop from L.A. was secretly cheering the audacious bastard on. To hell with national embarrassment—and that bit about police disgrace was just too damned bad.

What was *really* disgracing the cops, he knew, was not the fact that Bolan remained loose—the disgrace lay in the fact that Mack Bolan was doing the job which cops the world over could not or would not do for themselves. That was the disgrace. Bolan was a more effective cop than any of them, than all of them combined.

And they were going to kill him for it.

The mob had found somebody they could neither beat nor buy, and the guy was tearing them to pieces.

So, sure, what better police logic was there? Everybody had to have a weakness, every man had to have a price.

A man who could be neither bought nor beaten was a frightening thing in this society of legalized duplicity.

What was there left to do?

The cops would have to gun down Mack Bolan.

The guy was a goddamn national disgrace.

7: View from Ground Zero

Slowly and foggily, consciousness came. With it came an awareness of acute discomfort.

Her head ached. Her tongue felt twice its normal size and seemed to be mildly choking her. A threat of nausea trembled in her stomach.

Wherever she was, it was dark and damp there. It was also uncomfortably cold. The muted sound of a television set and an occasional murmur of voices came from somewhere beyond her range of vision.

Her arms and legs were either numb or paralyzed. Numb, she decided, remembering.

She was lying on her side, her cheek pressed against a hard and cold surface, with some evil-smelling and rough fabric draped over her.

A pained groan came from very nearby—and she remembered more of what had happened. Johnny, of course.

He was tied to her. They lay back-to-back, tied together at arms and legs with a harsh rope.

She fought her swollen tongue out of the way and whispered, "Are you awake?"

He groaned again, and she felt him struggling feebly against the ropes. Then his choked and frightened voice responded.

"Val?"

She fought back a wave of nausea and told him, "I'm okay. They've got us tied up, that's all."

His voice came back firmer; brave, a young edition of his brother's. "Don't worry, Val. Mack must know by now. He'll find us. Wow! My head is killing me!"

A vision of hypodermic syringes surged across her memory.

"They're keeping us drugged," she told the boy. "You have a hangover, that's all."

"I'll never get hooked on this feeling," he assured her, trying and failing to make it sound lightly humorous.

"Talk in whispers, Johnny. Don't attract their attention."

"Where are they?"

"Don't know. Somewhere close by, that's sure."

"Something stinks," he remarked, a moment later. "Smells like dead fish."

That was the odor, all right. She brushed her face exploringly against the fabric covering it, then abruptly moved her nose away from the contact.

"I'd say we're in a fish market, or a packing plant," she whispered. "They have us covered with old rags and gunny sacks."

"Ungh," the boy grunted. A moment later he asked, "Do I hear a TV?"

"Yes," she replied. "Another room somewhere, I believe. Johnny . . . are you alright?"

"Sure. But my legs are asleep. Look. Val. Don't be worried. Just keep telling yourself that Mack will be here soon. Keep thinking that."

Yes, keep thinking that. For all the world, she would not utter a word to dampen the boy's hopes. But Valentina Querente knew precisely why she and Johnny Bolan had been kidnapped.

They were merely so much bait in a trap, a lure to bring Mack Bolan inside. He would come, certainly. But he would come only to his death, and then the deaths of Johnny and Val would follow automatically.

Could this actually be happening?

Yes, of course it was happening. It was an event for which she had been mentally prepared since the beginning. The beginning of what? Of the nightmare, of course, the nightmare which had begun when she fell in love with a one-man army.

She was going to die . . . soon. And Johnny. And in the name of what madness?

It didn't matter, of course, why. The fact remained that they would die . . . with or without the intervention of Mack Bolan. So why take Mack down with them? Let him stay away . . . dear God, let him stay away!

Pray that he does not come, she wished to say to Johnny.

She could not, of course.

Instead, she told him, "Yes. He will find us. I'm not afraid."

But she was. It was not an intellectual fear, but an animal, emotional, trembling thing that kept lunging at her and expanding into her stomach and pushing against her diaphragm; an unreasoning terror which was trying to seize her mind and overcome her nervous system.

She was not, she decided, very brave.

A door opened and a soft light fell across her eyes.

The sound from the television set became louder.

Footsteps approached, magnified by the fact that her ear was pressed to the floor.

Another light came on, brighter, closer. A shadowy form was bending over her. The foul-smelling rags came away, and a man's face swam into her unsteady vision.

It was not a handsome face. But then, it was not a particularly evil face, either. Just a face. A young man, perhaps 28 or 30.

Another one appeared, peering down at her. This one was evil. It needed a shave. The mouth had a nasty curl to it. The eyes raped her. This man was older, in his 40's.

Both were expensively dressed but rumpled, as though they had not changed clothes for some time. She tried to study the details of these men, as though some forlorn hope had whispered to her that she might have to identify them some day, pick them from a lineup or a rogue's gallery.

The young man's face moved closer and he said, "Yeah, they're coming out of it."

"Told you I heard them," the other one said, self-pleased.

"The chick's feet are swollen up, George. You got her tied too tight."

The older one laughed nastily and replied, "Tough shit." He laughed again. "We got them tied wrong anyways. We ought to strip them both and tie them up face to face, belly to belly. That might get real interesting, next time they come to."

The other man chuckled and said, "He's just a kid, George. Probably wouldn't know what to do with it."

"He's old enough," the older one said with a nasty leer. "I bet he'd get the idea quick enough. Hey kid—want me to do you a favor?"

Johnny lay very still, apparently feigning unconsciousness. The nausea was again surging in on Val. She hoped that Johnny was genuinely unconscious.

Hands were running along her body. The older

man's voice found a level in her spinning consciousness. "That's nice stuff, damned nice stuff. Maybe I'll give the kid a lesson."

"Cut it out," the other voice demanded. "Skip said no funny stuff, and no funny stuff it's going to be. Not until he gives the word."

The evil one chuckled and said, "Well, just remember, I get first jump."

"If there's anything left to jump," the young one muttered. He was squatting beside her now. A hypodermic needle came into view.

She fought her mind to a standstill to plead, "Please, no more of that. I promise to be quiet."

The older man snorted. "Christ, she turns me on. That voice turns me on, Angelo."

"Shut up," the one called Angelo snapped.

He was studying her eyes, peeling back a lid for a closer scrutiny with a penlight, the way a medical doctor would do.

She said, "Please . . ."

He sighed and said, "Okay. But one peep and you get another jolt. Dig?"

She whispered, "I dig. Thank you."

He patted her leg, then traced a circle on her cheek and told her, "You're cold. Want some more cover?"

She said, "Not . . . not those rags. The smell is sickening."

"What would you do for a nice soft pillow and a warm wool blanket? Huh?" He made a vile suggestion, then laughed at the reaction on her face.

She was sick, physically sick, but she fought the retching and managed to squelch it, but at a terrible price in pain.

Both of the men were laughing at her.

The older one, George, suggested, "Stuff a rag in

her mouth, Angelo. She's gonna mess up the joint."

"Some loss," Angelo replied. "If she wants to lay in it, let her puke it up."

"Yeah, but *I* don't wanta lay in it," George said, chuckling.

Johnny lost his cool. He stiffened and began struggling against the ropes, muttering incoherent threats.

It was impossible for Val to see him, but she had a mental vision of that fierce young face, so much like Mack's, so stubborn, so proud and so outraged by human cruelty. She cried, "Johnny, don't, it's all right."

The younger man reached past Val's face to roughly rub his knuckles against the boy's head. "The kid don't like to hear this kind of talk in front of his girl, George," he said teasingly. "Wise kid, playing possum on us."

Val cried, "Leave him alone, please!"

"Just wait 'til my brother gets ahold of you guys," Johnny muttered, his voice muffled with frustration and anger.

George dropped to his knees beside the younger man and roughly gripped Val's thigh with one hand as he leaned across her to slap at Johnny with the other hand. "How would you like to eat your own balls, kid?" he growled. A string of obscene promises followed, including both victims, as he continued pummeling the helpless boy.

The other man was trying to pull him away, and Val was receiving knees and elbows as a result of the struggle. She tasted blood on her lips and tried to lunge away from a heavy knee in her abdomen—then suddenly both men were on their feet and the older man was being shoved toward the door.

"You crazy?" Angelo yelled. "Skip said hands off. Dammit, you keep hands off 'til he says different."

Tears of fear, pain, and outrage were pouring from Val's eyes, blinding her. The light went off, then the door closed, and again they were left in total darkness.

It was welcome, entirely welcome.

Breathing raggedly, Johnny said, "Val, I'm sorry . . . I mean, the way they treated you. Are you okay?"

"I'm fine," she assured him, choking on the words.

"Okay, just don't flip out. Mack will be here. And he'll make those guys eat every word of it."

Yes. Yes, perhaps he would.

Valentine Querente was suddenly coming into a deeper understanding of the man she loved, an understanding which she had once fought against.

She had disapproved of Mack Bolan's war . . . yes, right up until almost the present moment.

She had disapproved of the man himself, even while loving him.

No man had the right to take another human life, whatever the reasons. This had been her argument to Mack Bolan.

And he had tried to explain to her that there were men in the world who could not be regarded as men, who could not qualify as members of the human race. He had told her about the man-beasts, the social cannibals who prey upon the human society in utter contempt of all human rights and sensitivities, and he had tried to make her understand why he felt compelled to place his own life between these men and their intended victims.

She had loved him, but she had refused to understand.

It had not been a willful refusal. It was simply that

she had been unable to draw a mental concept of the savage men of whom Mack Bolan spoke. No human beings, she had thought, could be that vicious, that unredeemable . . . nobody had to *qualify* for membership in the human race. Humanity was a heritage, not an exclusive club for the specially endowed.

And so, yes, she had rejected the understanding of Mack Bolan and of his war. She had loved him, yes, and she had wept for him . . . but she had not found that understanding which justified the sort of man he had become.

But now that understanding was forming. It was forming against a background of terror, disgust and an overwhelming feeling of degradation, helplessness, pain and an overflowing revulsion.

Valentina Querente and Johnny Bolan were not the first human beings to find themselves subjected to this shocking state of helplessness and manhandling by men such as these. They were, undoubtedly, not the only ones receiving such treatment at the present moment. It was happening all over, everywhere, in one form or another, in every state of this land of the so-called free. And the police authorities were as impotent in the face of that other suffering as they were in this particular case.

Yes, Val was beginning to understand the forces which motivated Mack Bolan.

Those forces were outrage, frustration, a numbing and shocking realization that hordes of human cannibals were swarming this land and looting and raping it of everything decent and desirable . . . yes, they were robbing even essential human dignity and the right to be free from pain, fear, and intimidation.

In a sense, Mack had been fighting to protect Johnny and Val from the very beginning of his impossible war.

A much-overused cliché of World War vintage floated across her searching mind, resurrected probably from some gung-ho old movie on a late-late show: "I'm fighting so that my kids can grow up in a better world . . ."

Yes, Val was beginning to understand her warrior.

He was fighting for all the Johnnies and Vals everywhere, however corny that might sound. His own words to her, certainly not hackneyed, had been: "These people are a dripping, oozing mass of evil draped across the throat of this country. I'm going to pry them loose if I can, Val. Even if, in the end, the devil picks up all the marbles."

She had accused him of having a simple and uncomplicated view of the world. In her own naiveté, the simple and uncomplicated view had been her's . . . a view from an ivory tower, no doubt. There had been no shadings of good and evil; a thing was either right or wrong and there had been no rightful place in her exalted philosophies for killing, for taking a human life, whatever the provocation.

Well, the view from ground level was much clearer, even if dirtier.

But what did one do about human animals such as these, if they were able to corrupt and confound the laws of human communion?

Indeed, what *could* one do about them?

Mack Bolan, apparently, had found an answer. Perhaps it was not the best answer, nor even a moral one. But it was an answer. And, yes, the view was much clearer down here with the sufferers.

Yes, God yes. Find us, Mack. Not just for our own sake, but for the sake of human rights and dignity everywhere. In the name of all humanity, Mack Bolan, my love, *find us!*

8: Heat

Books Figarone had seen his share of living nightmares. He'd also had his full share of living in fear, of scrambling for survival. And he'd found out what it was like to be held up to public disgrace and humiliation, and to wonder if he would be spending the rest of his life behind bars.

Sure, he'd known it all.

But nothing like this.

There had been times when he'd suspected that death was lurking somewhere in the shadows and waiting for him—times when he could almost feel the heavy hand of fate weighing upon his shoulder—but no, hell no, there'd never been anything like this.

This goddam guy was death itself. This icy-eyed son of a bitch had nothing human in him that a man could appeal to. There was no handle there, no hope, not even a prayer.

The guy was *death*, and he had a way of creeping inside of a man and smothering him with that heavy knowledge. He even made the heart beat differently. He made the lungs try to stick together and slowed down the movement of blood through the veins.

The guy was death, and he'd sure been stuck with the right name. The *Executioner*, yeah—relentless, implacable, a law unto himself—and it was a law older than man's most ancient edicts.

Figarone had known some tough guys. He'd known some mean bastards, that's right, he'd known men who were nothing more than human sharks.

But he'd never known a man like Mack Bolan.

The guy never raised his voice. He never made any menacing or threatening gestures, never even used an angry word or tone. He didn't need to. He just gave that icy stare and handed out those cold pronouncements in a way that left no room for misunderstanding—and, yeah, you just knew that *death* was standing there and taking your measurements.

For over an hour, now, the lawyer from Cambridge had suffered the presence of *Mr. Death,* and he'd had time to formulate quite a few ideas regarding his captor.

And he'd begun wondering how the brotherhood had ever gotten a guy like this down on them. Figarone had heard all the stories, sure. He knew the legend of Mack Bolan. But, for God's sake, the stories didn't tell it all. Anybody who could sit and look at the guy for more than a dying minute or two would know that the stories didn't even begin to explain a guy like Mack Bolan.

So okay, the guy's family had been rubbed out. And he'd come looking for some atoning blood. So what was new? Things like that happened all the time—they happened right in the families, between some of the meanest sharks who walked on two legs. But nothing like that had ever produced a Mack Bolan.

This guy was . . . well, the guy was just something else. He didn't fit anything that Books Figarone had ever come up against, and Figarone was a lawyer who had long ago decided that he'd seen it all.

But there the guy stood—something new, something altogether different from the ordinary breed of men, and Books Figarone simply did not know how to handle the situation. There were no handles to reach for.

The guy was saying, "You ready to stop trying, Books?"

No, hell no. Books was not ready to stop trying. When he stopped trying, presumably, then he would begin dying. Presumably, hell. Figarone knew that he was living heartbeat-by-heartbeat. At any moment a big splattering bullet could erupt from that miniature cannon the guy was holding on him and Books Figarone was not yet ready to stop trying to avoid that impending event.

He sighed and tried to focus his eyes on the telephone list. It was close to midnight. Already he'd called just about every name in that book. As the list dwindled, so dwindled Books Figarone's chances for life.

He passed a hand across his eyes and told the big cold bastard, "Read that number for me, huh. My eyes are going out on me."

The death voice replied, "You should know that number by heart. If you're going to start stalling . . ."

Figarone hastily replied, "No, nothing like that. I got eyestrain, that's all. Who uh, what is that name there?"

"Sicilia," that voice announced.

"Oh yeah, sure, Harold the Skipper. Sure. I know Skip's number."

The guy was just standing there, spread-legged, the extension phone in one hand, that big silver blaster in the other. "So call him," he coldly commanded.

* * *

An extra television set had been rolled into the room and they were watching two channels at once, anxious to get the full story on the Middlesex hit. The television people seemed to be glorying in the whole thing. They were sure giving it plenty of coverage, from right at the scene.

None of the boys were saying much.

The whole thing was scary as hell, regardless of which channel you wanted to watch, and those announcers seemed to be trying to make it sound twice as bad, if that was possible, which Harold, the Skipper, Sicilia strongly doubted.

The telephone bell erupted into the tension of the moment, and Marty Corsicana, Sicilia's good right arm, scooped up the receiver before the second ring could come.

The boss of Chelsea divided his attention between the television special news reports and the man at the telephone as Corsicana growled, "Yeah?"

Then the Chelsea lieutenant turned a surprised gaze to the boss and tossed him the instrument. "Voice from th' grave," he announced.

The Skipper glared at the television screen as he jammed the telephone to his head and said, "Yeah, who's this?"

"Skip, this is Books Figarone," came the tense response.

Both of Sicilia's feet hit the floor but his eyes remained glued to the television set as he gasped. "God's sakes! We figured you for dead!"

"That's what I want to talk to you about, Skip."

"Christ, we all figured you was up at the Middlesex joint with the others. We thought for sure you was laid out on a slab somewheres! We give up trying

to call your house thirty minutes ago! Where are you?"
"Never mind. Listen, Skip, I—"
"Listen? You listen! Haven't you heard? That bastard Bolan made a hit on your joint up there tonight. It's all over television and everything. We been trying to get some words through our connections up there, but Christ, nobody is saying a damned word to us, not a damned word. Listen, that guy laid the goddam place low. I'm looking at it right now, on television—Channel, uh . . . hell, any channel, just turn your set on. There ain't nothing left up there, Books, nothing but a lot of trash and smoke. You're a lucky son of a bitch if you—"
"No wait," came the lawyer's agitated voice. "That's what I wanted to talk about. I *was* up there."
"What?"
"I was there. Skip, this guy is dynamite. Listen. I don't want to face anything like that again. We have to stop this."
"Well, yeah . . . sure, that's what I say. Uh, well, how many got away!"
"I don't know. It was hell, Skip, just sheer hell. The guy is worse than anything we ever heard about, I'll tell you that."
"Yeah, I . . ."
"I'm afraid that someone in this town has made a hell of a serious mistake, Skip."
"I guess I know what you mean."
"Listen. We have to cover this thing somehow. This guy Bolan has gone nuts. He's like a crazy man."
"Yeah, I get that idea."
"I'm sure that whoever pulled the snatch made an entirely honest mistake. You know. He thought he was doing the right thing, hell a beautiful thing. And it would have turned out that way except for one thing.

This guy Bolan won't play that sort of game. He's not a ransom guy. And now our engineer finds himself in a hell of a bad spot. His merchandise is too hot to be fenced. Nobody wants to touch it. Al 88 is just simply furious over the whole thing. The *Commissione* is furious. Every cop and police agency in the area is furious. And—the worse part, Skip, this guy Bolan is raging crazy furious."

"Why you telling me all this, Books?" the Chelsea boss asked warily.

"I'm simply interested in cooling the thing, Skip. If you're the guy, then hell, I want to help you."

"What makes you think I might be the guy?"

"I don't think anything of the sort. I'm just saying *if*."

A long sigh went across the wire. "Well . . . so let's say what if, then. What if I'm the guy? How would I go about getting out of this mess?"

"For God's sake, just turn them loose!"

"Well yeah, counselor, but that would be a dumb stunt, wouldn't it? I mean, what kind of advice is that? What if the pigeons could finger me? Have you forgot what the rap is for kidnapping?"

"That could be cooled, Skip. Hell, you know that. Anyway, that's the least worry you—our engineer could have. This whole damn town is about to explode around his head."

"Yeah, I get that feeling," was the worried reply. Another long sigh, then: "Well, if it was me, I think I'd just make a couple of cement suits and bury something at sea. I mean, if it was me had that worry."

"No! I mean, that would just make things worse, Skip. Our engineer must not harm those two people in any manner. Believe me, this is sound advice. He *must* release them whole and healthy."

"Well . . . listen, Books. I appreciate you thinking of me this way. And the other guy, too, the engineer. If I should run into him, I'll tell him what you said."

"Skip. Are you that engineer?"

"Hey. What the hell. That's no way to . . ."

"Listen, it's no time for tricky footwork. If you've got those people, Skip, you're in one hell of a mess. You'll have the entire organization on your neck. Al 88 already has crews of torpedoes swarming everywhere. And I hear that the gentlemen in New York have been in session all night. They're really upset by all this. They might be hanging paper down there right now—you know how excited they get at times like this. And to top it all, there's this Bolan running amuck like a crazy man. If something unhappy should happen to those two people, he's just liable to torch the whole damned town. And I don't know how you would ever explain your way out of something like that, Skip, even saying Bolan didn't get to you first."

Sicilia was patting his forehead with a balled-up handkerchief. He said, "Well what do you think I ought to do?"

"Do you have them, Skip?"

The boss of Chelsea was staring at the smoking ruin on his television screen. Presently he heaved a pained sigh and admitted, "Yeah. I got them."

"Where?"

"Never mind where. I got them in a tight place. I just wish I knew what the hell to do with them now."

The lawyer's voice came back sure and commanding. "Let me handle it for you. Where can I meet you?"

"I'm right here, Books," Sicilia replied uncertainly. "How come you want to handle it? How come you want to get your head on the block with mine?"

"It's already there, man. *All* our heads are on that block. I just want to get this son of a bitch off our backs, that's all. And I know how to handle it. Now where do we meet? I mean, you know, where's the hot stash?"

"You coming alone?"

"Don't you trust me of all people, Skip? Hell I'm—"

"How do I know you're not bringing Al the 88 with you?"

"On my oath of *Omerta*, Skip—hell, just use your own head. You've already told me you have them. Why would I continue screwing you around now, if I had something up my sleeve I mean?"

"You know where I keep my boat?"

The lawyer's voice tightened noticeably as he replied, "Up by Rockport, yeah. Is that where?"

"Near there. Listen. Meet me at the red wharf at two o'clock. Can you make that?"

"Yes, I believe I can make that. The red wharf at Rockport, two o'clock."

"Right. You come alone."

"You know I never go around completely alone, Skip. It isn't healthy."

"Yeah, well sure, but you know what I mean. One or two of your boys, sure, that's okay."

"I'll be there."

The line went dead. Sicilia slowly hung up and turned a sick smile toward Corsicana.

"Maybe I'm an ass," he told his lieutenant.

"I don't know, Books has always been pretty square," Corsicana replied. "What's he want to do?"

"He says we got to cool this thing down. He says the whole mob is raising hell about it. And Al the 88 is on the warpath. I knew that, hell he didn't have to tell me."

"So what's changed?" Corsicana asked.

"Maybe nothing," the Skipper replied. "Anyway we got a couple hours to think about it."

"What's there to think? I thought you already decided the thing had gone sour."

"Sure. But I don't want it to go from bad to worse."

"I still think we should heave them into Sandy Bay," Corsicana muttered.

"Maybe we will. But . . ."

"But what?"

"That wouldn't end nothing. That bastard would still go on helling around looking for them. Hid is hid, whether it's the shack or the bottom of the bay. Besides, I'm still not sure I want to let go of them just yet. Something might turn up yet."

"Like what?"

"Hell I don't know like what. All I know is, it was a beautiful idea, like Books said. Just beautiful. I'm not ready to write it all off yet. Maybe we could . . ."

"Yeah, boss? We could what?"

"Just, uh, never mind. We got two hours. Call Angelo and tell him we're coming out. Right away. Then get a couple of cars loaded. I'll think it over on the way to Rockport. You know something, Marty? I hate that bastard's guts. Bolan, I mean. I can't hardly stand the thought of just turning yellow and giving in to him."

"I know what you mean, boss."

"I just can't let him walk away from this with all the chips. I can't do it."

"You can't fight the whole world either, Skip."

"No, I guess I can't at that."

"So what are you thinking?" the lieutenant wondered.

"I'm not thinking, I'm weighing the catch. Now

shut up and let me weigh. I gotta understand what I got here. And you better get moving."

Corsicana grimly nodded his head and went to the telephone. He made the call to Angelo, then he went out to roust a couple of gun crews.

Marty Corsicana did not need to weigh anything, and he understood exactly what they had.

A bag of snakes, that's what. And there was only one thing to do with a bag of snakes.

Harold the Skipper should already know that, without weighing.

You took a bag of snakes and you chopped it up and you cast it in concrete and you dropped it in deep water.

That was the only understanding that would help this situation. The boss, Corsicana knew, would arrive at that understanding long before he arrived at Rockport.

There was only one way to handle a sour snatch.

Goddammit you destroyed the evidence!

9: Mafia Motif

Take a picturesque New England fishing village. Date its origins at somewhere in the early 18th century. Sketch in a couple dozen art galleries and an artist's colony numbering more than two hundred painters, twisting streets of picket-fenced colonial homes, and a jumble of antique stores and gift shops. Add a wave-lashed rocky shore with ancient wharves and sagging warehouses, screeching gulls, and here and there a cozy beach. Make its harbor busy with sportfishing boats, sightseeing cruisers and lobster fishermen. Give its more interesting parts colorful names such as Bearskin Neck, Motif #1, Dock Square, Front Beach, Granite Wharf, and Pigeon Cove.

Put it all together and call it Rockport, Mass.—and you've discovered one of the most beautiful spots on the American continent.

Artists, mariners, and merchants congenially rub elbows and constitute the stable population—or those who call the place home through good times and bad. Tourists by the thousands throng here during the summers, and some even brave the harsh New England winters to sample Colonial America at off-season rates.

And, yeah, even at one-thirty on a hellish morning

at the edge of winter, Rockport could be a nice place to find yourself. Bolan had been there once before, as a kid on a rare weekend at the seashore, and except for a new motel here and there he could find no signs of change to conflict with that sharply etched memory of a far happier time and visit.

According to Bolan's intelligence notebook, there were no Mafia activities here—not in any business sense. But Harold the Skipper was known to have a weekend retreat up near Pigeon Cove—and there was some interesting history connected with that fact which would not be found in the ordinary textbooks.

The underworld strongman of Chelsea had once operated a charter boat in the area for sportsfishermen —and once he had unsuccessfully tried to muscle a shakedown racket on the commercial fisherman of Rockport and neighboring Gloucester. That had been in the old days, when Harold Sicilia was just a small-time hood with bigtime ambitions.

He'd received his first big shot in the arm shortly after World War II when he negotiated a "disposal contract" with the Mafia bosses of Boston. The Italian Mob was in a big war with the Irish Gang at that time, with Boston up for grabs and the Italians grabbing harder and faster than the opposition. There were a lot of dead ex-enemies to be disposed of during that brief but very hot war, and talk around Greater Boston at the time had it that Skipper Sicilia was burying more bodies at sea than the U.S. Navy.

At a Senate Committee hearing on organized crime in the early '50's, a witness declared: "I'll bet you'd find more concrete at the bottom of Sandy Bay than you'll see around Boston Common."

No one had ever dragged the suggested area for evidence, but it was common knowledge that burial at sea had made Harold the Skipper a big man in local underworld circles. He had quickly expanded from the realm of mere disposal to the much more profitable field of murder by contract, completing the circle; his operation became a package deal, a murder-disposal monopoly which he parlayed into an ever-widening circle of encroachment into the local rackets.

When the acknowledged Big Boss of Boston, BoBo Binaca, abruptly disappeared from the scene, Sicilia moved in on Chelsea and proclaimed himself "co-ordinator" of all that moved and breathed in that city's underworld, as well as "enforcer" of all Greater Boston.

Nobody had contested Skip's claims to Chelsea.

But many neighborhood bosses in the Boston area openly dared the fisherman from Rockport to try any enforcing in their territories.

It was this situation, many observers felt, which produced the latest round of gang wars to plague the Boston area. Sicilia, forever the ambitious opportunist, had tried to move into the vacuum created by Binaca's disappearance and establish himself as the *de facto* boss of Greater Boston.

Others had different ideas.

Most notably, the national council of *Capo's* did not go along with Sicilia's designs. Enforcer maybe, sure—but under a man with some real stature. Harold the Skipper was admirably equipped to run the muscle franchise in Boston. But he was not a *Capo*. Moreover, he would never be a *Capo*.

Al 88 had been brought into the picture and his identity kept a carefully guarded secret, especially from the local contestants. And the national council had provided him with a force of gunners to equal Sicilia's elite cadre of assassins.

And then the Boston wars had started in earnest—but never as an open contest between *La Commissione* and Sicilia—things were not done this way. The old men at the national level believed in finesse. They would never openly challenge a local power or use obvious muscle to settle local disputes. The thing could always go sour. Their chosen opponent could emerge as a popular favorite of the locals, and that could lead to a very embarrassing situation. So the counter-war on Harold the Skipper was engaged in with considerable "finesse" and intrigue.

Sicilia, then, had backed down a little . . . but just a little. The tensions remained, Al 88's strong hand upon Boston remained, a surface peace developed, political connections were re-established and strengthened, new clout routes into the scandalized police organizations were quietly established . . . and through it all Harold the Skipper had cooled it, quieted it and awaited the next golden opportunity.

He sent his wife on an extended tour of Europe and tucked his only kid away in a private school, far removed from the sounds of warfare, then he gathered his forces around him like a protective shield and waited for a break.

Sicilia was not a particularly intelligent man, but he was a wily and a clever one—and he had good survival instincts. If the nationals did not admire Skip Sicilia, at least they had to respect him as a strong force on the local scene. This they did. And they also cooled it—and waited and watched.

The Skipper remained a marked man on the national level, however. He would not prosper, he would not grow and he would not live much beyond the duration of the present stalemate.

Much of this information Bolan gleaned from his

interrogation of Books Figarone during that tense 90-minute drive to Rockport. He also learned that several of the local bosses plus the mysterious Al 88 had early leaped to the conclusion that Sicilia was behind "the Bolan snatch."

Doubts had quickly arisen, though, that the Skipper from Rockport had the necessary "class" to execute such a flawless *tour de force* against the man whom all Mafiadom regarded with awe—Mack Bolan; and the final verdict held that Sicilia was not the engineer in question. Tentative investigations in that direction only served to confirm that feeling—and not even Al 88 was too keen on invading the fisherman's territory without a bit of firm evidence to back him up.

As for Figarone . . . he had been a popular arbiter between the Skipper and dissident Boston factions. He had, in effect, functioned as an unofficial *consigliere*, or trusted adviser, throughout the Boston wars. This, he explained to Bolan, accounted for the fact that the besieged neighborhood boss finally came clean with him and agreed to accept his "help" in this present red-faced situation.

Bolan was not so positive that Harold the Skipper had actually "agreed" to anything. The guy seemed to fit too close in a mold which Bolan had come to recognize as a classic pattern for street-corner punks made good.

They weren't so smart, no—in some cases, they were actually stupid—but these guys had come through the jungle of survival the hard way, and you could not simply charge it all off to luck. There was another force at work in the lives of such men, a jungle cunning combined with a total disregard for any rules, their own included—they lived their lives by ear, and they responded to an instinct which was as old as life on earth.

And they were very, very dangerous predators.

Figarone represented a different variety of Mafia mentality—the cold, shrewd, business approach to survival. A man like Figarone would carefully weigh alternatives and plot out a course of action, which—though as unconscionable and vicious as any—also contained certain elements of rational thought and logic.

Books Figarone had never been a street punk. He'd grown up in the suburbs, without the daily pressures of mere survival. He'd had the benefit of a good education, an exposure to the social graces, and he generally behaved as a respectable citizen—on the surface, at least.

The attorney had probably never pulled a trigger on another human being. His hands were "clean"—only his soul was dirtied, stained by scores of wrecked lives and ruined careers, and damned to hell by more sins against humanity than any book could record.

Of the two types, Bolan felt that the Figarone variety were far more dangerous to society as a whole. Not, of course, in a man-to-man fight. This type folded up quickly and stole away when violence began bouncing back at them. They had not learned the game of physical survival in an uncertain arena—and they had, in fact, no belly at all for such games.

Harold the Skipper would be an entirely different item. He would be hanging in there until the last gasp, until the final drop of blood had leaked out of him, and he would be fighting back all the while. That was the way of the jungle predator.

No . . . Bolan was not all that certain that Sicilia had "agreed" to anything.

And his blood ran cold every time he thought of Johnny and Val as being subject to the dubious mercies of a hood like Harold Sicilia.

Bolan had never felt a stronger challenge nor a more pressing cause. And he was more than a little uneasy about the new turn of events.

The rear seat and the trunk of the rented vehicle were loaded with a hastily acquired arsenal. There had been no time to transport his "war wagon"—a Chevy panel job fully equipped for *blitzkrieg*—to this new war zone.

Weapons were highly important to a one-man army.

They were the only difference that equalized the odds, that provided the hellfire beneath which he could wage an effective campaign.

And Bolan was not at all satisfied with the weaponry he'd been able to pick up on that hurried shopping expedition through Boston.

There was a bag of fragmentation grenades, a few smoke bombs, a package of incendiary flares, a couple of satchel charges which were too old to really be relied upon, a pound and a half of "goop"—plastics explosives.

He'd used up all the mortar rounds on the hit at Shot'n Feathers, and he'd abandoned the piece there.

He had the Beretta and the AutoMag hawgleg; he had the heavy chopper and a lighter machine-pistol—with plenty of ammo for all those.

And that was all he had.

It would have to be enough.

Maybe he would not need any of it.

Maybe it never snowed in Boston in the wintertime, either.

Bolan knew better. He would need every damned thing he could get his hands on, and more.

Harold the Skipper was not the kind of guy to simply give up and walk away.

Bolan could only hope that, from it all, Johnny and Val would walk away from it, whole and healthy, alive and happy.

But there was one hell of a cold ball nestling in the center of his chest, and he had learned to recognize the feeling.

Death was hovering close by. Death . . . and more than death. Hell itself was yawning, somewhere across the trail ahead.

Bolan knew it.

He, too, was a product of that human jungle . . . and he was a predator who preyed only upon predators.

And *that* required a motif of entirely another sort.

10: Madness

Bolan was at the wheel, Figarone perched tensely beside him and acting as navigator. They had not talked much during the preceding thirty minutes. Bolan had picked the *Mafioso's* brains of what he'd wanted; from that point he preferred the company of his own thoughts.

He had mentally reviewed all the events and intelligence of the previous tension-packed 24 hours, then he'd rechecked his conclusions and his angle of attack—and found not too much of comfort in the results. It was the best he had, sure, and the only way he had to go . . . but there was such an awful lot at stake here . . . this was not a routine hit on the enemy.

He would not—could not—entrust the safety of Johnny and Val to any third party or parties. It was not that he regarded himself as the only competent one in the field—it was simply that the thing was too delicate for casual handling. It had to be done just right—with just the right feel—and Bolan knew that no one else had his *feel* for the task at hand.

If Sicilia was still feeling tricky—and Bolan had to plan his own actions as though that were an established fact—then the guy could not be given a single option.

It had to be quick, decisive—and Bolan would have to hold all the aces.

He intended to do just that, if it were humanly possible.

A low overcast was lying over the entire area, and there was a darkness in that land such as can only be experienced on those remote New England coasts. A stiff wind was coming off the sea, and Bolan knew that it would be churning the surf and flinging it high into the rocks.

He had put the light topcoat on over his black suit and pulled a snapbrim hat low across his forehead. Tinted lenses in wire frames covered his eyes. For a few seconds, anyway, he could pass as a Figarone hardman.

And a few seconds were all he would need.

That was all it would take to jam the Beretta Belle into Sicilia's throat and offer him a quick alternative to sudden death. It would be the sort of alternative a man like Harold the Skipper would readily understand.

And that was the whole plan . . . as simple as that. At such a time, the simpler the better.

It was not, however, destined to work out quite that simply.

They had come in via Highway 128 to Gloucester, then onto Route 127, which entered Rockport as the main drag.

It was 1:30—they had arrived thirty minutes early, per Bolan's intent. At that hour the little village was rolled up and tucked in tightly. As they rolled on toward Dock Square, not another moving vehicle was in sight or sound. Only here and there did a light show from a dwelling. The street lamps along the square did little to dispel the heavy darkness.

Bolan sent the big sedan cruising through the square and onto Granite Street, the main coastal road. Just north of the village he turned around in the drive of a luxury motel which was closed for the season, then picked his way back through the village and onto South Street, moving casually in a quiet recon of the area.

By the time he eased to the curb just downrange from Motif #1, the famous red wharf, Bolan had a fair feel for the lie of this possible battleground.

The time was twenty minutes before two o'clock.

Gruffly, Figarone asked him, "Mind if I light a cigar?"

Bolan replied, "Go ahead. Do whatever you'd naturally do."

The lawyer got the cigar going, then he said, "You going to tell me what you've got in mind?"

"I'm going to grab the Skipper," Bolan told him. "Then I'm going to trade him his life for their's."

Figarone grunted. "Kill him when you've done with him. The others, too—all his boys. Otherwise your deal with me has no meaning."

"What deal?" Bolan growled.

The lawyer chewed furiously on the tip of the cigar for a moment, then he said, "You led me to a certain understanding. I expect you to honor that."

Quietly, Bolan informed him, "I led you to nothing. I give you the same lead now that I gave you then. I'll let you live awhile, Books. I'll let you live past me. But I'm not taking you on as a lifetime assignment."

"I don't need your whole lifetime," the lawyer muttered. "I just need a few more minutes of that willing gun of yours."

"My gun is not for hire," Bolan replied flatly. "And a few minutes could be my lifetime. I take it a minute at a time, counselor. Maybe you should do the same."

"That's a hell of an attitude," the attorney complained. "I put myself out on a limb for—"

"Knock it off," the Executioner commanded, the death voice sliding back into focus. "You put yourself on that limb twenty years ago—so don't start reminding me of my obligations. I'm trying very hard, in your case, to forget my obligations."

"Okay, okay," Figarone replied meekly.

"And I suggest that you breathe very carefully for the next twenty minutes or so unless you want a whole new deal."

The Cambridge boss chose to not respond to that suggestion. Instead he peered at the luminous dial of his wristwatch and said, "Skip could have gotten here by now. He lives only an hour away. I wonder what he's doing."

"Tell me again about the place at Pigeon Cove."

"Sure, well, it's just a shack now. Keeps his boat there. It's only a mile or so from here. He doesn't go there much, anymore, or so I'm told. Used to be a small warehouse for some lobster fishermen. Skip inherited the place from an uncle, along with his original boat. That's how he got into the business in the first place. I guess he keeps it now mainly for sentimental reasons."

"Or as a good place to stash hot merchandise," Bolan mused.

"Yeah, that too. If I had to guess, I'd say that's where he's got them. Or else on the boat. I don't understand why you don't just crash on in there and take them."

"It's no time to be crashing anywhere," Bolan said tiredly. "You remember that, too. You play it cool, Books—very damned cool."

"Depend on it," the lawyer murmured.

Depend also, Bolan was thinking, on me not crashing in any place where Johnny and Val could fall into the line of fire. There were better ways for such delicate missions.

The two men sat in silence for another twenty minutes.

At five minutes past two, Figarone suggested, "Maybe we should pull on up there, by the wharf. Maybe they're sitting back somewhere waiting for us to show first."

Quietly, Bolan said, "There hasn't been a car move in this town for half an hour, except this one."

"So maybe they got here first."

Bolan sighed, silently agreeing with the attorney. He cranked the engine and slowly moved the car along the curb until they reached the appointed rendezvous.

He left the headlamps on and the engine running, and he told Books Figarone, "Pray, counselor."

It had grown cold in the vehicle during the long wait, but the disbarred attorney from Cambridge was perspiring freely. He said, "You can't hold me responsible if the jerk doesn't show, Bolan."

Before Bolan could reply to that, another engine roared to life somewhere in that seaside village and squealing tires dug pavement in a fast take-off. Bolan decided that the vehicle was far up Granite Street, to the north.

Figarone laughed nervously and said, "See, they *were* waiting for us. Here they come."

Sure, here they came, but in too damned big a hurry.

Bolan had his window down and the Beretta nuzzled into the opening when the other headlamps flashed into view and swept down on their position.

He kicked his own lights into a rapid high-low sequence with the dimmer switch, as a recognition signal.

The other vehicle slowed, then squealed to a halt just uprange. The headlamps were on hi-beam and very nearly blinding, but Bolan saw a door quickly open and close—then the big car lunged forward again and roared down on them.

It swept by fast and accelerating with every horse at its command, but not so fast that Bolan and his nervous companion could not catch the shouted message left behind.

"So handle it!"

One of those frozen eternities elapsed, during which the Executioner's mind was freed from the dimensions of space and time to dissect and analyze and study over and over the implications of that heart-stopping moment—then his heart beat on, lurching somewhat in the certain knowledge of what he would find up there where that other car had paused so briefly.

A lump of something was lying at the side of the road up there, a something which did not move with life or even rustle in the stiff ocean breeze.

He eased the car forward until that bundle was directly under the headlamps, then he leadenly got out and went up for a close inspection.

The bundle smelled of long-dead sealife and something else—it was wrapped in foul and darkly stained rags and tied with a rough hemp rope.

He already knew what was inside that package, but he steeled himself and cut the rope off and peeled away the rags.

What he uncovered there was enough to send some men into insanity.

There was the headless body of an adolescent boy.

Both hands were missing, as were both feet.

There was not much blood, due probably to the method of dismemberment—and the unmistakable odor of seared flesh and burned blood lent testimony to that method. The remaining ragged stumps of neck, ankles, and wrists were blackened and cauterized.

The devils had performed the dismemberment with *a cutting torch.*

Entertwined with that mutilated body was another one in similar condition.

This one had once been a lovely young woman.

And it bore deeper indignities.

The breasts had been charred completely away.

Obscene words were burned into the torso, and the pubic mound was all but incinerated.

Bolan straightened abruptly from the inspection. A sound like a groan from hell passed through clenched teeth and he moved stiffly to the other side of the vehicle.

He opened the door and pulled Figarone outside, then shoved him to the front.

"There's your deal," the death voice intoned, only now it was death times ten. "Not even stiff yet."

Figarone took one horrified look and whirled quickly away from the grisly confrontation with Mafia methods.

"God's sake, Bolan," he gasped, "I had nothing to do with that, you know that."

"You do now," the iceberg tones informed him. "You stay with them. Get the cops out here, get a wagon. And you stay with them. If you don't, I'll be looking for you."

He was moving toward the driver's side of the car as he spoke.

The lawyer cried, "Don't leave me here! How will I—"

"You stay!" Bolan commanded.

He swung in behind the wheel and sent the car whining into reverse, then he whipped around and headed for the high ground of the cliff road.

A man could die a lot inside in just sixty seconds. And that was all it had been . . . sixty frozen seconds.

An automobile, however, could travel just so far in one minute. And from the high ground, Bolan could see those distant headlamps sweeping along the south coastal highway, the alternate route back to Gloucester—and he knew where he could intercept them, if he could get there in time.

He sent the powerful vehicle roaring into the pursuit, and as he settled into the grim business of piloting the hurtling car it was as though something inside of him separated into two parts—one already dead, the other raging to live and to kill.

Strange sounds were tearing up from the depths of him and he found his vision becoming clouded with unexplained moisture.

Then, in that curious division of consciousness, he realized that some submerged part of him was weeping—and the other part was saying, "That's okay, it's okay, sometimes a man has a right to cry."

Yet all the while he knew that the only thing commanding him at the present moment was the rage to kill.

Seldom had his war been waged in an attitude of anger or rage.

He was a methodical soldier, cooly dispassionate, doing a distasteful job, sure, but doing it just the same because it needed doing.

But now he was going to kill in anger, and he knew it, and he cared not a damn.

This was no longer a war.

It was not even a kill mission.

This was not the Executioner, moving methodically against an enemy.

This was Mack Bolan, brother of Johnny, lover of Val . . . and he was simply going to strike back at the rotten bastards who had done that to them.

Call it madness, okay, maybe that's what this weird double-consciousness amounted to . . . call it madness, call it anything, but Mack Bolan was going to get himself a monster.

And he was going to kill with pleasure.

11: The Reckoning

Angelo Scarpatta was wheeling, and he was in no great sweat now as they completed the loop around Cape Ann and straightened into the run along the south shore toward Gloucester.

George Ignanni was slouched in the seat beside him, guffawing with the delicious memory of what they'd pulled off.

Scarpatta growled, "Laugh, idiot. You'll cry tomorrow."

The older man chuckled and wiped at the moisture on his cheeks. "I can't help it," he wheezed. "I just wish I could've seen old Books' face when he unwrapped our little package."

Yeah, that had to be some scene, all right. Scarpatta would have enjoyed that himself. He felt himself loosening up, and he grinned and told his companion, "The counselor probably came unglued. He's probably sitting back there on the curb right now puking his guts out."

The other man howled at that and strangled on an aborted reply.

Scarpatta chucklingly added more fuel to the other's seizure. "Hell, he said he wanted to handle it, didn't he?"

Ignanni clutched his belly and tried to straighten

himself up. Tears were coursing down his cheeks and he was quivering all over. "The poor dumb shit!" he gasped. "What would he call that, Angelo? A *corpus delecti?*"

The wheelman laughed with his companion for another moment, then he sobered up and told him, "There's the golf course. We'll be off this rock pretty quick now."

"You ain't worried about Books chasin' us down, I hope!" the older man howled.

Soberly, Scarpatta replied, "Naw, he's probably flipping through his law books already, trying to see where he stands."

"Stop it," the other gasped. "I'm gonna get a heart attack."

"You ain't got no heart, George," Scarpatta told him, grinning.

"That's what *she* said!" Ignanni sputtered, exploding into another hilarious seizure.

Scarpatta really did not see anything all that funny. Books Figarone was no dumb shit. The guy was nobody to cross, not even when you enjoyed the protection of Harold the Skipper.

And this old sadist sitting next to him here . . . that sonuvabitch was sick, that's all. It was easy to see why Skip had warned him about that guy.

"George is an okay guy," the boss had told Scarpatta. "You'd never want a better disposal man. But you got to watch him, Angelo. You watch him until I give the word it's okay."

Sure, George was a crackerjack disposal man. But he was a jerk, too. He'd be laughing this one up for a long time, and Harold the Skipper ought to know how dangerous that could be. Not that Angelo gave a damn about what he'd done, that wasn't it. But Books was no guy to casually cross. Scarpatta didn't exactly like the idea of George the Geek laughing this one around. Not with the name of Angelo Scarpatta as part of the story.

He shrugged away the uneasy feeling and concentrated on the driving. Bass Rocks was just ahead. Should he cut up to 127 or should he take the dogleg on through to Interchange 9?

He was still wondering when the intersection warning marker came up. His foot lightly touched the brake, then he made his decision and again tromped on the accelerator.

An instant later the headlamps revealed a big sedan pulled across that intersection down there, lights out, just sitting there blocking the road.

Quick reflexes sent his foot again stabbing for the brakes as he yelled to his spluttering companion, "*Watch it!*"

Ignanni snapped out of his fit and was bracing himself with both big hands pushing against the padded dash as the heavy car laid a squealing trail of rubber toward an almost certain impact . . . and then something far more electrifying than a possible collision loomed up out of that darkness down there.

It was a guy, he was standing just a little to the side of the road, and he was dressed all in black.

One arm was up and extended at shoulder level and the biggest handgun Angelo Scarpatta had ever seen was suspended out there at the end of that arm and the goddam thing was blowing fire directly at him.

Even as the big rolling booms of that weapon were entering his peaking consciousness, Scarpatta was aware that his headlamps were shattering and going dead, that the front wheels were going into a wallowing rumble, that he was losing control in a sideways skid.

Ignanni screamed, "*Lookout, we . . .*"

Hell, didn't he know it, they were going to flip. Scarpatta leaned into the wheel with everything he had and prevented the careening vehicle from going into *that* roll, but then they were sliding around the front of the other car and going into a spin the other way.

Still that big pistol was booming and glass was shattering all around, showering the interior with flying splinters, and other slugs were ripping into the side of the car with loud thumps like somebody pounding it with a baseball bat.

Ignanni screamed and grabbed for his head, and then he became a displaced object as that swerving metal coffin heeled over to the driver's side, caught and hung on something, and then—like slow motion—gently overturned. The big guy was flopping all over the wheel for a moment, then the car just kept on going over and Ignanni was flung back the other way.

Scarpatta was held in check by his seat belt, and he sat there with both hands gripping the useless steering wheel as the vehicle completed a full roll and came to a shuddering rest.

Miraculously, it seemed, they were both still alive.

George the Geek was bleeding from a head wound and from numerous cuts about his face. Also, the flinging about must have broken or dislocated a shoulder, judging by the curious way he was sitting. The big guy was groaning and feeling of his head with one hand.

Scarpatta himself was not in bad shape, except that something had pushed in from the engine compartment or somewhere and had his legs pinned—he couldn't move them—also there was a helluva pain in his chest—from the steering wheel, probably.

The engine was still running but they weren't going anywhere. They were nosed into the embankment. The hood had popped loose and was skewed around, half off. Something flashed and sizzled up there, and Scarpatta had the presence of mind to quickly turn off the ignition.

He was a moment too late, however—already flames were licking up from the engine.

In a shaken voice, he told the other man, "George, that was Bolan I think! Snap out of it!"

But George was just holding his head and moaning, and Scarpatta couldn't move his legs. There was nothing wrong with his arms, though, and he was clawing for hardware even as he spoke.

Again, however, not soon enough.

The big tall bastard in black was standing there beside the shattered window, a huge silver pistol looking in on Angelo Scarpatta, and the Mafia murder specialist knew that something, somehow, had gone terribly, terribly sour.

He was gripped in some weirdly congealed state of consciousness and he knew it—that was the weird part, he knew it—but it was as though the human, feeling part of himself had received some sort of local anesthesic—it was like getting a shot of Novocain in the jaw, and knowing that you had a jaw but were unable to experience anything in that area.

The part of Mack Bolan that felt, that loved and hated, that grieved and rejoiced—that part was somehow mercifully anesthetized. He knew it, and he was glad.

In that part of him which was left in a sentient state, Bolan had known that he would overtake that other vehicle. He knew it because he would entertain no ideas to the contrary. With grim singleness of purpose he had hurtled along the inland route toward Gloucester, totally unopposed by traffic or other hindrances, and then he'd roared down to intersect the south coastal road just below Bass Rocks.

His route had been at least two miles and several minutes shorter than the torturous loop around Cape Ann. Even with their headstart, Bolan knew that he had them.

He'd beaten them by a full minute, with plenty of time to set the trap, and he had calmly stood there beside that windswept coastal highway and awaited the arrival of the prey.

He knew it was them the instant he spotted their lights. He watched the heavy crew wagon hunch down slightly as it slowed for the intersection, and he noted the quick decision and the sudden new acceleration as the wheelman decided to blow on through.

He knew the precise moment the guy saw the trap car—he knew by the sudden faltering of the forward motion of that speeding vehicle, and he noted with grim approval the desperate manner in which those brakes were applied and the big car started burning rubber.

And then it was AutoMag time. He raised the big .44 magnum and sent a pair of 240-grain messengers into the headlamps, following immediately with another pair into the front wheels.

That was all it would have taken, but he emptied the clip into them as they careened on past his position and went into the cartwheeling slide for the far side of the road.

He had but a flashing glimpse of something adrift and being flung around inside there as the mortally wounded vehicle screeched past the front bumper of his car and teetered into a roll.

Bolan coolly tracked the wreckage. He was standing less than ten feet distant when the slow roll ended and the crew wagon came to rest with all four wheels to the ground.

He snapped a fresh clip of heartstoppers into the AutoMag and closed immediately. The shattered vehicle was still rocking in the aftershock when he moved alongside and took a cool look inside.

It was a somewhat disappointing view.

He had expected to find Harold the Skipper in there.

Instead there was just a grizzled old hood with blood all over his face and a new-day's torpedo behind the wheel.

The wheelman was trying to haul out some hardware.

Bolan eased the AutoMag through the shattered window and lightly touched the heated muzzle to the guy's throat.

"Huh-uh," he commanded, the voice coming from some far-distant compartment of hell.

The guy's eyes rolled and he muttered, "Oh shit."

Flames were licking out of the engine compartment.

Bolan growled, "Where's Sicilia?"

"Sicilia who?" the guy asked in a strangled voice.

Bolan jammed the AutoMag harder against the throat and took a snubbed .32 away from the guy. "I got your package," he said. "Now I want the guy who sent it."

"Oh shit," Scarpatta again muttered. He was flinching away from the heated muzzle which was pressed into his throat, and his eyes were beginning to bulge. "Let me get out, huh?" he whined.

"Sicilia!" Bolan prodded.

"I don't know anything about any package!" The guy was coming unglued. "This thing is catching on fire! Help me get out!"

"*Sicilia!*" the Executioner insisted.

"Christ he went back to Chelsea, I think! Hey, my feet are getting hot, the damn thing's on fire!"

The big man at the far side was beginning to be aware of Bolan's presence. His eyes were glazed, almost crazed, gleaming like an animal's in the darkened interior of the wreckage. In a pained wheezing, he asked, "Is that the kid's brother, is that him?"

"Shut up!" Scarpatta gurgled.

The big man was struggling to get a hand inside his coat. He was saying, "Look, guy, you got the wrong—" when the AutoMag slid along the front of the younger man's neck and roared with an earshattering report, amplified even beyond its normal thunder by the enclosed space.

Scarpatta's head jerked back as though it had been spring-loaded and his eyes nearly lunged from their sockets. The big hollow-nose bullet was not intended for him, however; it smashed into the ear of George Ignanni and blasted on through and out the other side, carrying with it a collapsing skull and a frothy mixture of blood and brains.

Blood was flowing from Scarpatta's nose and he was doing odd things with his lower jaw, working it up and down and side to side. The thunderous recoil of the big pistol, in such close proximity to the

Mafioso's head, had evidently jarred things loose up front as well as rupturing the eardrums.

The guy was probably blind and deaf, and he was screaming piteously as he told Bolan, *"It's burning, get me out, I'm on fire!"*

"So burn," Bolan growled, remembering two others who had died hideously by the flame.

He was stepping back and quitting that place when the gasoline vapors ignited and flames whoofed along the entire length of the vehicle.

The guy back there was screaming bloody murder, and Bolan was several paces removed when some feeble signal freed itself from anesthesia and rose up to rebuke him.

He whirled about and raised the AutoMag, sighting directly into the screaming, flame-wreathed mouth, and he sent unearned mercy into there, and the screaming ended in a bubbling gasp.

He said to the sighing night, "Chelsea, eh?"

He returned to his vehicle, then Mack Bolan—brother of Johnny, lover of Val—took his numbed mind on to the next stop along the hellfire trail.

12: Night of Nights

One effect, certainly, of Bolan's numbness—or quite possibly the cause of it—was to shut out any mental reconstructions of the hideous last few moments in the lives of those pitiful turkeys he'd left behind in Rockport.

Later, those reconstructions would inevitably come, with grievous pain and with probably an even deeper shock to the mind of this man.

Bolan, after all, was intimately familiar with the ways of his enemies.

They would have done the boy first. They would make the woman lie right there beside him and listen to the agonized shrieks and they'd try to make her watch as they torched off pieces of him—a hand at a time, a foot at a time. And if the shock of that piecemeal slaying had not catapulted the boy into merciful death or unconsciousness, they would have gone right for his throat while he was still screaming.

The things they'd done to *her,* the hideous mutilations to the body itself, they would have done before they started cutting her up. If they'd been particularly sick, then they'd have done it slowly and carefully, trying to keep her awake and aware throughout the ordeal—they'd want her to know what they had done to her particularly private parts before they went on to the routine stuff.

Yes, Bolan knew his enemies. He knew what some of them were capable of. Indeed, what certain mentalities among them gloried in. Even some of those who were not particularly sick, in any clinical sense, would have taken a delight in doing to Bolan's loved ones what they would prefer to be doing to the man himself—as though by substitution of victims they could get even with this hated enemy.

Bolan, of course, regarded himself as solely responsible for what had happened. It was his lousy war, and the hatreds which had been inspired by it, which were to blame for the present sorry state of things.

There were a lot of "beloved dead" on Bolan's backtrack and these weighed heavily on the mind and the conscience of this man. Johnny and Val were merely the final, crushing blow.

Yes, the numbness of mind was serving a purpose . . . and Bolan perhaps understood this, even though he moved about like a man in some strange trance, even though he knew—at some subliminal level of consciousness—what it was he was being insulated from.

These things could be threshed out later—if there was to be a later. For now, the mood was sufficient unto the moment. It was a mood for destruction, and he knew where to find those who were deserving of his attention. He had, in fact, an intelligence notebook crammed with directions to the front.

Less than an hour after the grisley experience at Rockport, and while the police were still at the scene and questioning a contrite and humble Cambridge lawyer, the man in black turned up at the Chelsea residence of Arturo "Fat Artie" Mariotto, a lieutenant in the Sicilia organization.

It was a fairly modest two-story older home on the north side of Chelsea, undistinguished in a neighborhood of similar homes. Mariotto lived there with his wife of twelve years and two small children. His business activities, which included prostitution, organized extortion and shylocking were carried out from an office in the basement.

Bolan apparently knew all this.

On this night of nights, Mariotto had sent his wife and children to stay with relatives in Arlington, a northwest suburb of Boston, but this fact Bolan could not have known—and perhaps this accounts for the quietness of his initial probe into that hit-site.

He left his vehicle at the curb a half-block from the house and closed on foot, wearing the light overcoat and a snapbrim hat.

The neighborhood was quiet and dark, with light coming only from the Mariotta residence and even this was muted and inconspicuous.

Bolan turned up the walk and went directly to the front door. He rapped lightly, received an immediate response.

The door cracked open and a cautious voico inquired, "Yeah? Who's that?"

"Santa Claus," Bolan growled. "C'mon, let me in."

The doorman flipped on the porch light and was trying to get a look at the caller.

In an impatient tone, Bolan demanded, "C'mon, meathead, don't put me in no goddam spotlight, f'Christ's sake!"

The door closed and the porch light went off.

Bolan heard the rattling of a chain-lock being released, then the door opened wide and the guy behind it greeted the Executioner with: "Can't be too careful, y'know. Not tonight, of all nights."

Bolan agreed with him as he pushed on inside.

The guy told him, "They're downstairs."

"He send Harriet and the kids away?" the caller inquired.

"Yeh, you know it," the doorman replied, still trying to get a good look at Bolan's face.

He did not.

Perhaps the last thing in all the world this soldier saw was the chilling black snout of the Beretta Belle's silencer, perhaps the darting little flame that sighed out from it. The nine-millimeter slug thwacked in directly between his eyes, and the guy very quietly died on his feet.

Bolan helped the body down to a silent fall, then he quickly scouted the main level of the house.

He came upon another hardman sitting at the kitchen table, staring sadly at an empty beer bottle.

Again the Belle whispered of death. The rear man slumped quietly across the table.

Bolan went upstairs then, and quickly satisfied himself that no one was there.

He returned to the main level, found the door and stairway to the basement level, then he went down to join the party.

It was not much of a party.

The basement room had a floor area of about 200 square feet. The lights were too bright and the air too polluted. Four guys were sitting around a card table, none of whom bothered to look up when Bolan entered the room.

Fat Artie was seated in a swivel chair a few feet further along, gazing with heavy-lidded eyes at a small television screen.

Bolan announced his presence there with a marksman's medal, which he tossed into the pot at the card table, and the Belle sighingly executed the foursome while they gawked at the new table stakes.

Mariotto swung the chair around and lunged to his feet in an amazingly fast scramble, considering his weight problem. He was trying to bring an oily Army .45 to bear on his most urgent problem when the whispering Beretta cut his hand away from it.

The fat man fell over against the wall and stayed there, panting and holding the shattered hand to his chest. Twice his eyes met that icy gaze of Bolan the Enraged, and twice the gaze faltered and fled to less upsetting views.

From Mariotta's viewpoint, the big guy was just standing there, those legs spread, the shoulders leaning forward slightly, the black blaster poised there like a cobra ready for the strike, and he was saying nothing—absolutely nothing.

Presently Fat Artie gasped, "Well whattaya want?"

The guy said nothing.

Mariotta nervously tried again. "I got nothing personal with you, Bolan."

Personal or not, his blood was leaking all over the floor. He licked his lips and said, "I guess I'll just stand here and bleed to death, eh?"

Funny, it didn't really hurt much. Just numb, sort of. Artie had always heard that. Big wounds never hurt that much. Get a hangnail, now, and you'd go outta your skull. But something like this, and . . .

The guy wasn't talking. Course not. He hadn't come to talk, that's why. He'd come to listen to Artie Mariotto talk.

"Hey, uh, I don't blame you a damn bit. I'd be

pissed off myself. I mean, I'm a family man. I know what you're being put through.

Still nothing, no reaction whatever. Just standing there, staring.

"Uh, I told Skip he shouldn't screw around with a man's family that way. But what the hell. Skip's the boss, I'm not. Look, Bolan. Do I look like a guy would do a rotten thing like that, snatch some guy's family? A fat man like me? Hey, I wouldn't . . . I mean, I just ain't built for that kind of stuff."

Nothing.

"God, I guess I'm just going to stand here and bleed to death, huh? Look, he's not going to hurt them. He promised me that. I still told him to deal me out, I didn't want any part of a thing like that. Hell, Bolan, I got all the damn territory I need, I don't *want* anymore. I told Skip that. He's got these crazy ideas of taking over the whole town. Hell, he's crazy. But, Bolan . . . he ain't *that* crazy. He's not going to really hurt your family."

Quietly, surprisingly, Bolan asked, "Where is Sicilia now?"

"God I don't know, I swear. I been trying to get him myself for two hours. On the phone, I mean."

The guy was just staring again.

Mariotta tried to squeeze off the bleeding, and he tried Bolan again. "He's got this crazy idea, Bolan, that's all. He *wanted* you to come roaring to town. God, I swear. He thought you'd take out after this here Al 88 we got now. Know who I mean? Listen, I *told* him that was a crazy idea. Look, I just run a few girls and I got a few quiet little deals turning here'n there. I don't go for this rough stuff. I'm a family man. I sure wouldn't go for a snatch just to taunt a guy with."

Softly, the big guy said one word. "Pawns."

"Huh? Naw, I do a bit of uh, you know, personal loans. But I don't do no pawn business."

"How old are your kids?" the tall man asked in a strangely soft voice.

"Eight and ten," Mariotta replied hopefully. "Uh, no eight and *nine*—Patty don't have her birthday 'till next—"

Bolan said, "For them, then," and he spun about and went out of there.

Fat Artie was perhaps the only Chelsea area *Mafioso* to face Mack Bolan on that night of nights and live to tell about it.

In the succeeding two hours, Bolan blitzed a path across that north Boston suburb which left, by the most reliable count, 52 dead men strewn in his wake.

He destroyed a pool hall and a cafe, burned two nightclubs to the ground, rousted the girls and torched five houses of prostitution, and knocked over a syndicate "bank" in the city's eastern section.

At a few minutes before dawn, Chelsea's choicest residential neighborhood was rocked by a series of shattering explosions which reduced to rubble and ashes a reputed quarter-million-dollar home owned by one Harold Sicilia.

And, by the dawn's early light, a harassed and weary-eyed group of law-enforcement officials met at the scene of Bolan's latest strike to hear an irate police inspector declare, "This guy has gone bananas. He's ripping through this town like an enraged rogue elephant, and you've goddammit got to stop him! I don't care how you go about it or what you have to do, but I want you to stop this crazy bastard!"

The tenor of the inspector's demand was perhaps influenced by the unsettling fact that several of the sites which had been subjected to Bolan strikes had been under police stake-out at the time.

"I'm putting the whole city on overtime," he fumed. "Nobody goes off duty, nobody gets sick, nothing else gets done until we stop this fruitcake son of a bitch!"

One of the listeners was Leo Turrin. He was wearing dark glasses and his coat collar was turned up to nearly meet the brim of his hat.

The fact that he was present, in this gathering of top police officials, indicated or rather emphasized the seriousness with which the law-enforcement community viewed the situation.

He turned to a companion, a dark-featured man on crutches, and woefully commented, "He's not crazy. That's the worst part. He thinks those poor turkeys they dropped at Rockport were Johnny and Val. The way to stop Bolan is to somehow get the word to him."

The other man replied, "We're broadcasting it on everything at our disposal. It would be much better if we could actually produce those two, alive and well."

The speaker was Harold Brognola, an official of the U.S. Justice Department who had arrived on the Boston scene a few hours earlier. He added, "I doubt that anything else would deter him now. Trantham could be right, maybe he is over the edge. Bolan is not the cold death machine that everybody tries to make him. The guy has a heart, after all, and every man has his limit. Maybe he *has* gone temporarily insane. All the blood tests and bone samples and other physical evidence in the world may not be enough to convince him that those bodies could not have belonged to Johnny and Miss Querente. We've simply got to produce the *people*, Leo."

"Yeah," Turrin said sadly. "But what if we only turn up a couple more turkeys instead?"

"I wish," Brognola replied testily, "to hell you had not said that, Leo."

"I just wish to hell Mack would contact me," Turrin muttered. "I've got ears out everywhere, I just wish he'd drop a word."

"Yeah."

"Listen, if Figarone was leveling with you, Hal, then Sicilia is the crazy one. He pulled the dumbest stunt I ever heard of. If Mack had any restraints before, it was mainly the fear that he'd overrun Johnny and Val, so he was moving very carefully. Now that he thinks they're dead, hell . . . there's nothing to restrain him. He won't stop until he's dead or there's nothing left around here worth hitting."

"That's exactly what I'm afraid of," Brognola replied, sighing.

The little undercover cop lit a cigar and puffed it to a high glow, then he glared at the charred embers of the Sicilia mansion and declared, "Screw Trantham! I'm not shedding any tears over what he's doing to the mob here. That's not crazy, that's just Bolan in rampage. Hell, he hasn't hurt anybody else yet, and I'm betting he won't, even if he goes completely off his rocker."

"That's the whole problem, Leo," Brognola murmured. "It's something we can never be sure about."

"Yeah, well, what I'm interested in is getting word to the poor guy. Sure he's half outta his mind. Who wouldn't be? I'd just like for him to know that what he saw up there at Rockport was *not* Johnny and Val."

Indeed, Mack Bolan would have been a far happier and saner man if someone could have reached him with the truth about Rockport.

The night of nights had ended, yes, but a furious

new day was just beginning . . . and a rampaging young warrior was still beating the hellfire trail in search of Harold Sicilia.

Even the truth would not have significantly altered the course of events at Boston, however. Regardless of who the hapless victims should turn out to be, *some* two innocents had served as stand-ins for a grisly game of horror, and Mack Bolan had seen the results. No, the game plan would not have been significantly altered by the truth.

And, yes, Bolan was in rampage.

Wherever he paused, death fell; wherever he lingered, hell descended.

And the most thoroughly shaken and rightfully frightened man in Greater Boston was at that moment counting the costs of his ambitions and wondering what he should do now with his "hot merchandise."

He still had the hot pair, yes, alive and negotiable.

The paramount consideration now was simply this: How could he best use them to ensure his own continued good health?

The answer to that perplexing question was not within the intellectual reach of Harold the Skipper Sicilia . . . and his street-jungle instincts had gone bankrupt.

A showdown was brewing, and Sicilia must have known that he had run out of options.

But, as Bolan had guessed, this was a guy who would fight to the last gasp, to the final drop of blood.

For Johnny Bolan and Valentina Querente, the night of nights had not yet met its dawn.

13: Day Two

It was eight o'clock on the morning of Day Two in Boston. The major commuter highways into the city were under peak load in the early-morning traffic hassle. On the Northeast Expressway, a major route which carries the brunt of the daily population shift in the northern areas, a speeding vehicle with four grim-faced men aboard was making excellent progress in the lighter traffic of the outbound lanes. The vehicle was a month-old Continental, and the man behind the wheel was driving like a professional.

At a point just inside the suburban city of Revere, a community bordering Chelsea to the north, another vehicle moved smoothly alongside the Continental and casually paced it through two interchanges.

Witnesses later reported to investigating police that the second vehicle seemed to be "maneuvering" the Continental, over a course extending for several miles, and that the men inside that doomed vehicle appeared to be highly agitated throughout that period.

The driver of a parcel-service van admittedly "chased" the strangely behaving vehicles, "trying to keep them in sight," and this witness reported that gunshots were exchanged between the speeding cars throughout that wild last mile.

Another witness, however, insisted that all of the

shooting was coming from the Continental—that the lone man inside the "pursuit car" did not open fire until the very end.

Most of the following traffic had fallen back to give the dueling vehicles plenty of room; those ahead quickly made room and remained clear. Many regarded the bizarre incident as a police chase, but none within sight or sound of the contest could have been unaware that something unusual was taking place.

At a point where off-highway congestion became minimal, in more or less open country, the chase car suddenly veered over to "bump" the other vehicle from the side, and this is the point where most witnesses agree that the first firing erupted from the pursuing car.

"You could tell the difference," a Navy CPO reported. "The earlier shots were all coming from ordinary guns, like maybe thirty-eights. But when the other guy opened up, hell it was like the booming of a shotgun. I was maybe a quarter-mile behind them at that time, but hell, I *knew* when that dude starting laying into them. And it was obvious why he waited so long. You see, he was trying to maneuver them into the clear. He didn't want to hit them back there in all the congestion."

"That dude" was, of course, Mack Bolan. The men in the other vehicle were later identified by police as "mob torpedoes—some of the new bunch that we've noticed around town lately."

All four in that vehicle were dead of gunshot wounds, undoubtedly while the big car was still in forward motion. The chase vehicle "stayed right with it, just sort of guiding it down and keeping it nudged over against the guardrail. When it stopped, he stopped. And then *I* stopped, damn quick. I could see then that the guy wasn't no cop. He was dressed in this skin-tight outfit, all black, and he looked like he was ready for war. The other traffic was going on around, but I didn't. I knew who the guy was by now, hell I couldn't hardly believe it at first, I mean I actually *saw* the guy, you know, pulling off one of his hits.

"No, I wasn't worried. I was right behind, so I just pulled over and sat there watching. Some other cars had pulled in behind me, but most of them were going on around, rubbernecking, you know, but going on around.

"The guy was pulling those bodies out of the car and going through their pockets. And he shook that car down good, I mean he even opened the trunk and looked in there. He was looking for something, bet on that.

"Hell, he was going about it just cool as hell. He wasn't worried about cops or anything, I guess. Would you be? If you was that guy? He just calmly shook everything down, then he walks around the rear of the Continental, heading back to his car, and he kind of paused there for a second as he was getting in and looked back at me.

"Yeah, he looked right at me. Hell I just sat there and looked back. He didn't look like what I would've thought—in the face, I mean. You know, he didn't look like a killer. He just looked tired. Yeah, tired as hell, and maybe sort of sad.

"But can you *imagine* that guy. He chases this car along a busy expressway, shoots all four of the goddam guys dead where they sit, then maneuvers that big Lincoln to a rolling stop with his own car—and not another damn car got involved in it—you know, nobody else got hurt. I call that amazing."

The foregoing eyewitness report was given to a television newsman and recorded at the scene. It was typical of other stories gathered at the same time.

Later that morning, Leo Turrin was to privately comment, "Crazy, huh? Stampeding blindly, huh? Bull! It's the same old Bolan. A little madder, maybe, a little deadlier. But it's the same old Bolan. I say leave him alone. He knows what he's doing!"

Indeed, it would appear that the blitzing warrior knew precisely what he was doing. Less than an hour following the incident on the Northeast Expressway, he made an appearance in the offices of a telephone-answering service, in a building just off the Boston Common.

According to the supervisor there, he was wearing a business suit, shirt and tie, carrying a light topcoat draped across one arm.

"He seemed very tired. His eyes were dark-circled and rather bloodshot. He very quietly and politely told me who he was and what he wanted. I told him that I could not give him information from my files. I also told him that he should call the police, that it was all over radio and television about the mixup in Rockport.

"He seemed stunned, and he made me repeat it twice. All I could tell him was what I'd heard myself that morning. I'm not sure that he believed me. Anyway, he insisted on going through my files and I wasn't inclined to argue with him. It was sort of sad, anyway. He's a beautiful man, you know, truly beautiful. I don't believe all the stories I've heard about him.

"Yes, he took some information from my files. No,

I don't know what he took. When he came in he was holding a little black notebook. It had dark stains soaked into the pages, like blood. He was referring to some numbers in the notebook while he searched our numerical cross-index records. He jotted down information from several of our cards and replaced them in the card file. He thanked me as he left.

"No, I have no idea what he was looking for. We have hundreds of clients. We also have a mail-forwarding service, you know.

"Yes, he checked those files also. He was here for about ten minutes. Frightened? Of course not. I told you . . . he is a beautiful man."

At sometime between nine and ten o'clock on the morning of Day Two, Bolan entered an office building near the new Federal Center and invaded a suite of rented offices on the 14th floor. According to the building management's records, the tenant was "A. Montgomery Enterprises"—but no such business was licensed or registered with the Commonwealth of Massachusetts, the City of Boston, or any of the trade associations.

"A. Montgomery," it later developed, was actually one Alonzo (Hot Al) Mantessi, a syndicate enforcer with a national reputation. He was not directly associated with any of the local Mafia families, and apparently he had come to Boston several months earlier with a sizable crew of sharp-dressing and "classy" torpedoes.

Bolan left behind him at A. Montgomery Enterprises six classy carcasses, including that of Hot Al Mantessi, now Cold Al. Each of the men met death via one or more 9 mm slugs in the head. Desks in the offices had been ransacked, and a small safe in Mantessi's private office had been blown.

At 11 o'clock that morning, Bolan established contact with Leo Turrin, by telephone. He told him, "I'm hot on the trail of Al 88. Is it true about Johnny and Val?"

A greatly relieved and concerned undercover cop assured Bolan, "It's true. That's not them, Sarge. The guy pulled a switch on you, but I can't imagine why."

"I can," Bolan replied. He sounded weary and wrung-out, but a hint of fire remained in that voice. "He didn't want *me*, Leo—he wanted Boston. And I think I know the only option left for him. I'm tracking it now, and I'll try to keep you posted. I'm hoping the trail will end at Johnny and Val."

"We're talking about Skip Sicilia now, right?"

"Right," came the tired response.

"You sound like you're at the edge of death, buddy."

"Pretty close," Bolan admitted. "I've taken a couple of hits in the flesh and I've lost a bit of blood. But I'm okay, so don't start fussing."

"Put it down, man."

"Can't. I'd take a nap if I thought I'd ever wake up. I've got to keep on it. Now that I know . . ."

"Yeah," Turrin said, understanding that unfinished statement. The time element was as important as ever, with Johnny and Val still in the picture. He told Bolan, "Weatherbee cracked the thing at the Pittsfield end. Sort of ironic. Want to hear how Sicilia tumbled to Johnny, or do you already know?"

"No, tell me."

"Talk about your small worlds. Sicilia sent his wife to Europe and his kid to a private school some months back. Guess which school he was hiding the kid in."

Bolan's weary sigh carried across the distance. He said, "Okay, I guess that ties it up pretty well. I guess Johnny and the Sicilia kid got to know each other."

"Worse yet, they were close buddies. Each had a secret, bursting to be told. You know how those things go."

Bolan replied, "Yeah. I know how it goes. Okay, Leo. Thanks."

"For nothing," the cop said ruefully. "You're, uh, okay now?"

A quiet ghost of the old Bolan chuckle came across the wire. "I haven't lost my springs, if that's what you mean."

"Well you had a lot of people worried. Be careful. Trantham has you on a shoot-to-kill alert. He thinks you've gone bananas. And, uh, Brognola has hit town."

"How's his leg?"

"Fine and so's his temperament. Mack . . . he really didn't have his heart into that Vegas thing."

"Yeah, I know," Bolan replied wryly.

"But you watch it. This town is primed for you."

"I'll watch it," Bolan assured his friend. "Uh . . . , Leo . . . who were they? The . . . uh . . . people at Rockport."

"Erase it."

"Can't. Who were they?"

"A Chelsea prostitute. Skip probably grabbed her on a sudden inspiration, took her up there with him. The boy hasn't been positively identified yet. But a kid is missing, up that way. An uh, retarded kid, Mack."

Turrin heard soft swearing, then Bolan said, "Well, let's contact every hour, okay? It's getting close now."

"Will do. You're still tracking Sicilia?"

"I'm trying a bit of reverse English."

"Whatever that means, eh," Turrin said. "Never mind, I don't even want to know. But you'd better shift gears down to a slow crawl . . . if you intend to see this thing through to the end."

"Yeah. Talk to you in one hour, more or less."

That was the end of the conversation.

Bolan, however, was not "shifting gears" downward. If he was shifting at all, it was from deadly to deadlier.

He had new life blown into him, new hope . . . and he had a new angle of attack.

Day Two was to be the final day of the Boston blitz . . . but that day had very barely begun.

14: Reverse English

Geographically speaking, the city of Boston is far removed from the center of the nation. Historically and spiritually, though, Boston is actually where it all began and could be regarded as the ovum of the American dream. It was from this successful colonial settlement at the northeastern edge of North America that the torch of liberty flared out to engulf a continent, to change the maps of the world, and to alter the course of human history.

Boston Common, likewise, is not the geographic center of the city—but any discussion of "the cradle of liberty" must and does begin right here in the oldest public park in America.

British troops once camped here. Less than a hundred years later, Civil War soldiers pitched their tents on the same ground. Pirates were hung here, as were "witches."

Directly north of the Common rises historic Beacon Hill. The citadel of Victorian Boston, fabled Back Bay, lies directly west. Just north and east stands the magnificent new Government Center, a sixty-acre complex of modern buildings, plazas, and malls—on the same ground which sailors and other adventurers of many generations once knew as Scollay Square.

For the Boston visitor, the Common is the starting

point for that historic backtrack known as "the Freedom Trail"—a colorful trek along the landmarks of the spirit of '76.

For Bolan, the Common was merely a reference point from which to travel another kind of freedom trail—in his own language, a "nerve path"—and the track led him along Beacon Street to the western edge of the Public Gardens, down to Commonwealth Avenue, and into Back Bay.

At one time Back Bay had been one of the more fashionable residential sections, with more blue blood, acre for acre, than any plot of land in America. Many of the nineteenth-century town houses of the early Boston aristocracy now serve as rooming houses or apartment buildings. Some have become institutionalized and preserved, while others have been restored to their original elegance and maintained as upper-crust family residences—and it was upon one of these latter that the Executioner had set his sights.

The name of the guy who lived there was supposed to be Albert Greene . . . but Bolan knew better. It was Alberto Guarini. He was supposed to be a reputable financier and a respected "patron of good government" in Boston, a civic godfather no less—but again Bolan knew better.

Guarini-Greene was as vicious a shark as had ever rippled the surface of American society . . . a syndicate trouble-shooter with unlimited reach and unrestrained sprawl . . . and he had been assigned to these troubled waters to gather in all the little fishes which seemed to be slipping through the voracious Mafia nets.

He was known in some quarters as Al 88.

The guy had more than a code name . . . he had an entire code life. He'd come to town and married that

Back Bay house, via a desperate widow and a crumbling family which had plenty of Boston pride and little else.

Guarini had "restored" the family right along with the mansion. He'd even taken their place in the social register, their civic honors, and all the prestige that accompanied the package.

But he had not accomplished all this in the space of two short years.

According to the intelligence brief which Bolan had worked up on the guy, his infiltration of the genteel set had started more than ten years earlier.

Guarini had spent much of those intervening years trotting around the world on missions for his masters, while at the same time establishing a "legit" reputation as an international financier at home base.

He wasn't the kind of guy you'd find at an "Appalachia meet" or in a smoke-filled conference room at some hardsite.

He would not pack hardware, nor would anyone around him.

There would be no way to tie the guy to any mob-dominated interests. He was "legit" all the way, Mr. Class himself, the respectable face to be worn as a mask by the international association of goons and hoods around the world.

He was a guy who could lunch with kings and presidents, bankers and industrialists; yeah, and he was a guy whose name could appear on directorial boards of important foundations and institutions—it was a name which could influence economic barometers, civic undertakings, and national-level politics.

Yeah.

It was even a name to stand in the forefront of a "reform" movement toward better local government.

A guy like Guarini-Greene would use only about 10 percent of himself in direct syndicate operations, and even that heavily covered. Of course, that 10 percent was the tail that wagged the rest of the dog. The other 90 percent was sheer front, a facade from behind which the ugly face of international hoodlumism could appear at a critical moment to gobble up some choice unsuspecting tidbit or to annihilate some threat to its masters.

So, sure, many of Guarini's involvements with the outside world, in fact the bulk of them, could be viewed as entirely legitimate and respectable—even, perhaps, laudable. This was necessary if the guy was to be an effective trouble-shooter when those critical moments arrived.

But that whole 90 percent of solid respectability was nothing but fuel for the flames with which the syndicate meant to roast the world. And Alberto Guarini, alias Albert Greene, alias Al 88, was a 100 percent rat.

Bolan had a bit of trouble connecting a guy like Guarini with the "Al 88" operation. It was not the usual assignment for a bigtime front man like Guarini.

Something big . . . something really *big* must be at stake in Boston. Something that would be felt far beyond this spawning ground of the American Revolution—yeah, something rotten was definitely brewing beside the cradle of liberty, and it did not smell to Bolan's sensitive nose like anything which boded well for the American nation as a whole.

Manhattan was the national nerve center in the financial sphere.

Washington was the political center of the nation, maybe of the world.

But what was Boston?

Bolan would think about that, and wonder about it at more length, at a better time. For now, a rescue mission was on tap . . . and Bolan meant to involve Al 88 in that project.

Yeah. The mob had screwed up, they'd played their ace as a deuce. They should never have compromised the big man in this way.

The guy just wasn't built for such games.

Maybe he was a mystery man as far as the cops were concerned; maybe even the local *Mafiosi* had never caught a sniff of the guy.

But Bolan's jungle instinct had led him straight to Back Bay and Al 88.

An Al 88 type of operation could not operate without muscle. "Hot Al" Mantessi had provided that muscle . . . and very briefly Bolan had wondered if the coincidence of names—Al 88 and Hot Al—contained any significance. He had quickly dismissed the idea, however. Hot Al could not possibly also be Al 88. Hot Al was an enforcer, pure and simple—a "classy" one, sure, but any order of enforcing was a very limited role for an entirely limited mentality.

Al 88 was the "finesse" man, the brains behind the Boston takeover—and the "brains" had to have an access route, a nerve path, to the "muscle."

Finding that nerve path had been no terrible task . . . not for a searcher who was not straitjacketed by legal restraints.

Business contacts between the two Als had been accomplished via the telephone-answering service, and Bolan had quickly ridden that path directly to the "brain"—and now here he was, looking at the skull itself.

It was a nice-looking joint. Large, impressive, the cream of Boston society had probably entered those doors upon one occasion or another—generations of it.

And now the Executioner was going to do so.

His ring brought a response from an honest-to-God English butler, an Arthur Treacher type in living pallor and all done up in tie and tails.

The guy sighted along his nose in a manner which was probably supposed to discourage pests and unsolicited guests, and he chilled the air about Bolan's head with a haughty, "Yes?"

Bolan shoved the guy out of the way and stepped inside, kicking the door shut behind him. "Mrs. Greene," he said coldly.

Bolan had to give it to the guy, he had a good supply of cool. The eyes shifted blankly from the visitor to the closed door and back to the visitor again before he asked, "Whom should I announce, sir?"

"You should announce Mack Bolan," the Executioner quietly suggested.

Living Pallor's face went even paler and the eyes twitched a bit, but he waltzed smoothly about and led the way along a richly paneled hall and to impressive double doors which he opened with a restrained flourish, like opening the doors to a kingdom.

"If you will wait in the library, sir," he buttled in that starched British voice.

"No, I guess I'll tag along with you," Bolan told him.

The guy didn't like the idea, but he was no dummy. He went through the ritual of closing the double doors, then he led Bolan to the rear of the house and into a pleasant room with plenty of glass along the back wall.

Seated in the sunlight at a small table was a fragile woman of perhaps 45. She had been very beautiful once, and in fact, probably still was during her best moments.

This was not one of those moments. She wore no makeup and she was clad in a simple print smock and furry slippers.

She was having breakfast, at a time when most people were thinking about lunch.

Bolan felt a surge of pity for this delicate goldfish who'd taken to swimming with sharks. He had to wonder just how much she actually knew about her husband's activities. You could fool some of the people some of the time, but not all of . . .

The butler was making an apologetic announcement. "Terribly sorry, Madam, the gentleman insisted upon being shown in immediately."

She was looking at Bolan without curiosity, without any visible emotion at all. In a voice of quiet refinement she asked him, "Are you a policeman?"

Yeah, she knew a little.

He replied, "Not hardly. I'm Mack Bolan."

Something flashed deep within those murky eyes, but here was a woman who had been trained throughout a cultured lifetime to look pretty and smile in the face of the most devastating emotions.

She said quietly, "Won't you sit down, Mr. Bolan? May I offer you some coffee?"

Bolan declined both offers. The butler decided to leave them in privacy; Bolan also declined that courtesy. "Stay," he commanded softly.

Then he asked the woman, "Do you know why I'm here, Mrs. Greene?"

She shook her head with that slight tilting motion taught at young ladies' finishing schools and told him, "No. Should I?"

He told her, "Your husband is a Mafia front. His

real name is Al Guarini, also known as Al 88. Are we on common ground now?"

The cool eyes were examining her coffee cup. Ignoring the rest of the declaration, she replied, "Al 88? How novel. Yes, I suppose so. My husband could have been a concert pianist, Mr. Bolan. He is a master of the 88 keys."

Bolan said, "I'll bet he's great on death marches."

Without lifting her eyes, she asked him, "What do you want, Mr. Bolan?"

"I want the safe delivery of two human beings who are very dear to me, Mrs. Greene. I want my brother and I want my girl. You tell that to Al 88. You tell him that I intend to have them, and all in one piece."

"I see," she replied quietly.

"If I don't get them, and very quickly, I'm coming blitzing all over his neat little Boston front. Tell him that."

The woman's eyes remained transfixed to her coffee cup. In that fragile voice she asked the Executioner, "How much time do we have, Mr. Bolan?"

He did not overlook the "we."

"Only God knows that," Bolan told her. "I recommend that your husband move very quickly if he wants to save the day."

"All right," she told him, raising the eyes to his gaze. "Thank you for the advance notice. I will deliver your message."

"Fine. Tell him this, also. Hot Al is now very, very cold and so are all his boys. So we can deal directly now. It's down to him and me. Tell him that."

"Yes, I understand."

Softly, he said, "You've been expecting me, haven't you?"

Her face confirmed what her voice would not. A

variety of emotions surged around on there, erasing the training of a lifetime, before she quietly announced, "I love my husband, Mr. Bolan."

He replied, "I'm sorry to hear that. Your husband is an enemy of everything you should believe in."

In a barely audible voice, she replied to that. "Yes, I know."

"Tell him," Bolan commanded gruffly, and he spun about to leave.

"Mr. Bolan!" she called after him.

He paused at the door. "Yeah?"

"How do we . . . contact you?"

"He'll figure out a way."

He went on out then, and the butler glided along behind.

The guy held the front door for him and followed him to the stoop to say, "Good day, sir. Smashing, that was simply *smashing*."

Bolan grinned soberly, said, "Thanks, I call it reverse English," and he went away from Back Bay.

That took care of Mr. Class.

Sicilia the Slob was next on tap.

15: Pat Persuasion

Bolan contacted Leo Turrin and told him, "Okay, I've rattled a big cage. Keep your nose in operation. If you start smelling heavy feelers, protect yourself but react quickly. Don't expose yourself to anybody in this town, though, I mean not *anybody*."

"You think someone will be feeling for a meet?" Turrin asked.

"Unless all my feel is dead, Leo, someone will be pounding on hell's door for a meet."

"Okay, you'd better tell me about it."

"Not yet. Too delicate at this stage. I want no muffs, so the less you know the better. If the word comes along, though, play to it. Go ahead and set it up. I'll agree to anything reasonable. Just don't expose yourself."

"Why all the—?"

"I'm going to drop a name on you, Leo, just a name, and just in case things go sour for me. You can take it from there. Okay?"

"Okay. Drop."

"Guarini, Alberto."

"Never heard of him."

"Sure?"

"Sure—no, wait. There was a Guarini in the old . . . but no. That guy died ten years ago."

"Were you at the wake?"

"No, but I—what are you saying? What does Guarini have to do with—?"

"That's the full drop for now, Leo, sorry. I leave you there. Now you cover yourself."

"Pretty, uh, pretty big?"

"You know it."

"Well wait."

"Get Brognola to check it out for you, if you must have details now. But very carefully."

"What the hell, Mack."

Bolan sighed heavily. He said, "Something big is brewing, Leo. Probably has been for a long time. I'm beginning to understand why the nationals are so shook up over this snatch. But listen, Leo. I want Johnny and Val. That's number one. After they're in the clear, well . . . then I'll cooperate all I can in this other thing. Just play it by ear and try like hell not to over-react to anything you see or hear. If someone big—I mean someone up high, now—tries to set up a meet with me, you see that it gets set up. I want nothing to scare the guy away, nothing to take away my bargaining edge. And that means, buddy, no damned prying and snooping around my big man's heels until I'm done with him."

"Okay, sure. Hell, you know how I feel about all this, Mack."

"There could be people around this guy, I mean sympathetic people with a lot of influence. So don't expose yourself. Don't let the guy get that close to you."

"I got you."

"Okay. What else have you got?"

"You're sounding better."

"I'm feeling better."

"You should be. Here's what I've got. Chelsea is in a state of shock. The backlash from your blitz has already started up there. The Chelsea cops have made over fifty arrests in the past two hours, guys they should've had behind bars years ago. The clout palaces are crumbling. They're rounding them up *now*, before you take it into mind to visit again, I guess."

"Sounds great."

"Yeah. I hear other municipalities are beginning to think in the same direction. And there's panic in all the clout palaces, everywhere in the area. The shock waves have traveled clear to Providence. People down there have empaneled a special grand jury, and they're handing out indictments up the kazoo."

"Sometimes a gentle nudge is all it takes to move the ball," Bolan commented musingly.

"Yeah, well, that's not exactly any gentle nudging you're doing around here, buddy."

Bolan pushed a tired sigh along the line and said, "I'm glad to hear about these developments, Leo. But what can you tell me about Sicilia?"

"Sorry, not much. Coast Guard finally found his boat. It had been run aground up in Ipswich Bay, just around the horn from Pigeon Cove. Bloodstains all over, but all of them match up with the, uh, turkeys from last night."

Bolan shivered. "Okay. Thanks. That takes care of the facts, eh?"

"Yeah."

"Okay. Now let's have the odors."

Turrin sighed. "Don't go on the blitz again, Mack. That's a gentle suggestion from an old friend."

"Might have to. What do you have?"

"There are movements. All around. The factions are getting together. Mutual protection, I guess, the herd instinct. A guy by the name of Hoops Tramitelli is re-organizing the army. Know him?"

"I think we met, sort of."

"You did. He was the head hardman at Middlesex last night."

"Okay, yeah, I make the guy."

Turrin said, "Way I hear it, you're number one head on their list. Sicilia is number two."

"Yeah?"

"Yeah."

"And what do you hear about Al 88?"

"Not a murmur. You wiped out his whole damned hard force, Sarge."

"You'll be hearing from him," Bolan muttered.

"I will?"

"I'm betting somebody's life on it."

"Okay. Uh, Guarini is Al 88. Right?"

Bolan sighed. "Yeah. With a legit cover. Watch it, Leo. Play it very cool."

"Hell, you know it."

"Okay. Talk to me again in two hours."

"Will do."

"A minute, Leo. What'd they do with Figarone?"

"Took his statement, released him. He played it pretty straight, Mack, from what I could gather. I guess you instilled the fear of something higher than *omerta* in him."

"Good. Thanks, Leo."

That took care of one loose end. Bolan hung up and consulted his notebook, then made another call.

Ten rings were required to bring Books Figarone to his telephone.

The voice was weak and irritable. It said, "Okay, who's that?"

Bolan told it, "Thanks, counselor. You played it straight."

"Christ! Leave me alone, Bolan! What the hell do you want of me now?"

"I hear your buddy Hoops is rounding up a head party."

"I wouldn't be a bit surprised, but I know nothing about it."

"I thought you might want to get the word to Skip," Bolan said.

"I don't get you."

"He's number two on their list, right behind me, and I guess you know why. And I was just a little surprised to find *you* at home, counselor."

"Surprised why? What do you mean?"

"Well, they . . . what the hell, I guess I'm wrong. Forget it."

"Wrong about what? Forget what?" The guy was starting to sweat. Bolan could almost smell the perspiration through the telephone.

"Just something I heard," he replied lightly. "Probably nothing to it. Forget it, you've had your time in hell. I just wanted to thank you for staying with those bodies, even if they weren't who I thought they were."

"Now just a minute, Bolan! What the hell are you talking about? What have you heard?"

"It's just . . . what the hell. I told you they've got this hard on for Sicilia now."

"Yes, yes, I can understand that. But what . . . ? You started to say something about . . . Does somebody have a hard on for me too, Bolan?"

"Well, yeah, I guess they would get ideas like that."

Bolan could feel the sweat dripping all over the floor around Figarone's telephone.

"You mean just because I . . . ? You mean, they'd think I was . . . ? Aw, no. Hoops and all the boys know me better than that. They wouldn't think . . ."

Bolan said, "Sure, you're right. You have nothing to worry about, so forget it. Get some rest. You deserve it. You sound pretty tired. I guess, uh, you have pretty good locks on your doors and all, eh?"

"Hey what the hell, Bolan! What're you trying to do to me? Are you just . . . ? Or is there something you're not telling me, I mean *really* something. After all, I put my head way out on a limb for you last night. And I even waited right there with those stiffs, and answered all those questions. I followed your wishes to the letter. I gave a complete statement. Now if you know—"

"Well sure, that's just it, I guess. I guess the boys got the idea that you were just a bit too cooperative. I guess they figured you had a lot to cover up. You know."

"Jesus Christ, Bolan!"

"Hey, relax. They're your friends, right?"

"That's no Goddamned comfort! You know that!"

"What the hell are you yelling at me for, counselor?"

"This is all on your account! I want some protection! I want—"

"Hey, relax," Bolan broke in soothingly. "The best way to cool this thing is to cool that hot merchandise. Right?"

There was a momentary silence, then: "So that's it. You're trying to set me up for another try."

"Guess again," Bolan said. "I'm already working another angle. I just called to say thanks, counselor."

"What other angle?"

"Al 88."

"Oh. What, uh . . . ?"

"We have this understanding. Either he delivers the hot merchandise, cool and happy, or I rip up his cozy little cover operation."

"Oh . . . God! You know his identity?"

"I do."

"Well that's . . ." A whole new tone was edging into that voice now. "That's a little hard to believe, Bolan. The guy is so well covered, even *we* don't know who he is."

"Too bad for you," Bolan said easily. "The guy is right now sitting up in Government Center demanding that you and several other well-known figures get put out of business. He's blaming this whole snafu on you boys in the north. He's saying it was all set up between the Middlesex Combination and the Sicilia Gang. And he's putting the pressure on all your clout routes, he wants you disenfranchised, all of you."

"Why should I believe that?" Figarone sneered. "From *you*, of all people."

Casually, Bolan said, "Go to hell, I don't care if you believe it or not."

"Well what . . . ? Why would he do a thing like that to me?"

"He's doing it very seriously, I mean with national approval. The old men want this area cooled. You guys are messing up a hell of a big operation, I mean a big *national* operation. If this doesn't work, I hear they'll probably hang some paper. You know."

"Why tell me all this? Simply looking out for *my* best interests are you, Bolan?"

The Executioner chuckled dryly. "Course not. Look, Figarone. All I want is my kid brother and my girl. The rest of you guys can go to hell in a basket for all I care."

"What are you suggesting that we do?"

"You're the *consigliere*. You figure it out. But if I were in your shoes, I think I'd want this area cooled from my own efforts. You dig?"

Bolan heard the snap of a lighter and the sucking sounds of a cigar being coaxed to life. Then the Cambridge lawyer asked, "What would be the best way to go about that, Bolan?"

"Get those two people back to me. That's all it takes, Books."

"I don't have the faintest idea of even where to begin, and that's the truth."

"You begin with Skip Sicilia."

"Big deal! If I'd known where Sicilia was, I'd have strangled him with my own hands hours ago."

"I'm going to start blitzing again in one hour, Books. I'm going to hit everything from Haymarket Square west, and that means I should reach Cambridge somewhere around three o'clock. I'm going to shake your Goddamned town to pieces, then I'm going to Charlestown and Somerville, then I'm going to circle back through Medford, Malden, and Everett. Have you heard what's happening in Chelsea right now, Books?"

The counselor had heard. His voice was shaky as he told Bolan, "A rampage like that would be crazy. What's that going to prove?"

"It'll prove that the heat is still on. Good-bye, Books. And I sincerely mean this . . . good luck."

"Wait dammit, Bolan wait! What can I do?"

The guy was practically wailing.

"You get with Al 88. And you get with Sicilia. That's what I'd do. And I'd set things up between them, for an exchange of prisoners. I mean it. That's the only save you've got left."

"How would I . . . ? God's sake! *I* don't contact Al 88! *He* contacts *me!*"

"I have the phone number, Books. It's an answering service, but the message will get there." Bolan read off the number. "Got that?"

"No, wait while I get a pencil—hell, please don't go away, I'll be right back."

Bolan was not about to go away. He waited until the thoroughly aroused Cambridge boss returned to the line, then he read off the number again.

"Okay, I got that," Figarone panted. "Where the hell do you pick up stuff like this?"

"Here and there," Bolan replied. "I'm sorry, I don't have anything on Sicilia. Except that he's not on his boat. It's been found."

"Oh."

"Yeah. So I leave it with you right there."

"Where'd they find the boat, Bolan?"

"Ipswich Bay. It'd been run aground and abandoned."

"I see." The attorney was regaining his composure. "All right. I'll do my very best."

"You'd better."

Bolan hung up, pocketed his notebook, and returned to the battlefields.

It was time for another punch or two at the city's pressure points.

16: Deadline for Death

As mementos of the Northeast Expressway hit of the early morning, Bolan had a rather bothersome groove along the front of his right thigh, and a thin patch of hair and scalp had taken leave from the top of his head.

The U-drive vehicle was carrying a couple of bullet holes in the door and all of the side glass had been shattered. He had cleaned away the mess and was running without windows.

He had not seen a bed for going into the sixtieth hour, and food had become no more than a vague memory.

His guts had not come unchurned since he first learned of the disappearance at Pittsfield, and he had lived with the constant vision of Mafia turkeymeat lurking at the threshold of his thinking mind throughout that period.

He was weary, soul-sick and he had already slain more men than he liked to think about since his arrival in Boston.

But he had to get out there again, and he had to blitz. He had to keep the pressures on, had to keep hitting and hitting until the rats had scurried their way totally out of options . . . he had to make them come to him, humbly and repentantly, with two olive branches held tenderly forward as evidence of that repentance—two olive branches named Johnny and Val.

He began the next round of hard persuasion at a lottery drop near Haymarket Square. There he executed a couple of small-timers who were no strangers to the Boston police.

Within ten minutes of that strike, he had hit two other mob hangouts in that same district and bloodily closed the police files on several more well-known citizens.

Then, while police sirens shrieked in all directions about his line of travel, he crossed the Longfellow Bridge into Cambridge and deposited a swath of hellfire through that sedate community, knocking over two "powder factories"—wholesale distribution centers for hard narcotics—a loan company specializing in "vigorish" loans to students, a used-car sales lot which was actually a fencing operation for stolen vehicles, a call girl "agency" which had lately been recruiting local coeds—and a bar and grill which, by some strange coincidence, was a hangout for mob figures and off-duty policemen alike.

The Cambridge blitz was climaxed by a personal visit to the offices of a student newspaper—a brief "interview" with the Executioner by an agog staff, and a list left behind tersely identifying mob activities and the men behind them in the Ivory Tower city.

And at three o'clock, Bolan again made contact with Leo Turrin.

"You were right," his ally told the Executioner. "A concerned citizen here by the name of Albert Greene is making all kinds of noises about cooling this quote slaughter unquote. He's climbing the walls over at

Government Center right now and demanding that quote something fresh unquote be initiated."

Bolan had read the guy pretty well.

He said, "Okay. Is anybody listening?"

"Everybody's listening," Turrin replied. "The guy is owed a lot of favors around this town. He's in the mood to collect now."

Bolan commented, "Okay, that's just what I wanted."

"I've . . . uh . . . had the ear and the sympathies of Hal Brognola."

"So?"

"So you're pretty cute, aren't you. Hell, he poked a long-distance program into the computers in Washington and come up with some damned amazing stuff. How come it takes a million-dollar computer to tell us something you already know, Sarge?"

Bolan said, "I actually know very little, Leo. It was about 90 percent hunch."

"Well your hunches are batting a thousand. This fucking Greene or Guarini or whatever you want to call him—this guy has even dined at the White House, Christ's sake. This is dynamite, absolutely scary damned double-dynamite. Brognola is shaking all over. I've never seen the guy like this."

"I hope he's playing it cool," Bolan muttered.

"*Cool?* Try *frozen*. Some of his own goddam bosses could be involved with this guy, Mack, unwittingly or otherwise. If I hadn't been sitting right there when the stuff was ticking in, I'd have never caught a peek at it. I know that."

"That bad, huh?" Bolan commented glumly.

"Yeah it's that bad. This is the kind of stuff that topples governments, my friend. You can come up with some of the damnedest . . ."

"That's not the top of my mind right now, Leo."

"Oh yeah, sorry."

"What's new at the front?"

"Well, I told you, you were right. The guy wants a meet."

"Okay, when and where?"

"Not so damned fast. There are conditions."

"I accept the conditions."

"Without even hearing them? Here's the set. Greene is volunteering to act as go-between between you and the quote hostile forces unquote. The object, of course, is to arrange the release of Johnny and Val and to get you the hell out of this town."

Bolan said, "Okay, so far."

"He's posing as a concerned citizen who simply wants to cool the war here. Now he's engineered a moratorium—not a pardon, now, just a moratorium. The cops will not bother you if you will agree to the conditions, and if you promise to behave yourself in the meantime. They'll remain clear and allow you to negotiate the release of prisoners."

Bolan said, "Damned nice of them."

"There's more. You'll meet with Greene at the center of Boston Common. You'll be guaranteed safe passage, in and out. There will be no cops around the Common, and in fact they will establish a buffer zone to guarantee absolutely no accidental police interference. But you've got to knock off the war in the meantime. No more of that crap like at Haymarket and over in Cambridge."

Bolan said, "You've heard about that, eh?"

"Me and all of Boston. The TV stations are breaking in on scheduled programming to keep the town informed. This is all very embarassing to the fuzz, buddy. One radio station has started referring to them in editorials as quote the Toonerville Cops unquote."

"That hasn't been my intention, you know that," Bolan muttered. "People shouldn't blame the cops. They're not equipped for this kind of war."

"Yeah, well, they'll get over it. They've been called worse things than that in this town."

"When is the meet?"

"Midnight."

Bolan said, "No."

"That's not negotiable, Mack. And Greene didn't set that requirement. The Public Safety people insisted on it. They're going to make sure the park area is cleared out, and they say it's midnight or after, period."

"Midnight is too far off."

"It's not negotiable, Mack."

Bolan sighed. "Okay. Maybe it's for the best. Maybe a bit of cooling will get these people to thinking more clearly. Okay. I'll meet him at midnight. Tell him to bring Johnny and Val with him."

"What? I don't believe—that wasn't in the deal, Mack. His story is that he will talk to you and get your terms. Then he will try to communicate those terms to the other side."

"There are no terms," Bolan said tiredly. "He knows that. He's just trying to cover his own tracks. Tell him to bring them with him. I'll give him until midnight to bring them in. Give him this, for Sicilia. I'll call it a fair trade, their flesh for his. I'll call it even."

"Well . . . okay."

"That's the deal, Leo, the only deal. It gives him nine hours to produce Johnny and Val. Give him this message, also. If they are not there, safe and sound, at midnight . . . if they are not there with him then I don't even go in. Instead I blow the whistle on everything I know about the mob routes into this town and out of it. I'll write Johnny and Val off as dead. And I'll turn him and his operations here into hamburger. You tell him that. He'll know what I mean."

"Well . . ."

"That's the whole deal, Leo. I want it plainly understood what's at stake, so you see that he understands completely."

"Okay," Turrin said, the voice thinning out a bit. "I guess you know what you're doing. But you may be giving the guy an impossible task. You should understand that. I mean, with so much at stake on your end."

"I understand it. A guy who has the moxie to get himself a dinner seat at the White House, Leo—don't you think he should be enterprising enough to handle a hood like Skip Sicilia?"

"Maybe you're right. But, uh . . ."

"But what?"

"Why do you want him to bring them to the Common, Mack? Wouldn't it be better to have them turned over on some neutral ground? Let him have them delivered to the cops, to a hospital, anywhere that's safe."

"No. I'll have to see them with my own eyes. I may not be able to walk away from this one, Leo."

"I—uh, yeah, I see what you mean. Okay. I'll deliver the message. You'll have to honor the conditions, Sarge. No more war during the moratorium period."

Bolan said, "Okay, I'll give them that much. They'd just better deliver, that's all. I'm through playing button-button. They'd better understand that. Midnight is the absolute deadline. If I'm not happy by then, the whole damn cookie crumbles. Be sure he realizes that."

"He'll understand it."

"Thanks, Leo. Your cover still tight?"

"Yeah."

"Does, uh, Brognola know that you're talking to me?"

"Oh sure, unofficially."

"Okay. Let's keep it that way. Leo . . . If I don't walk away . . ."

"You will."

"If not . . . get them to a safe place."

"You know I will."

"Yeah, I know that. Okay. To seal the deal, I'm becoming unavailable. No more talks until midnight, and that's the end of the road."

Bolan hung up and massaged his weary eyes with both hands.

Yeah, the end of the road.

It had been a brutal one.

He just hoped that midnight was a deadline which would make it all worthwhile.

If not . . .

If not, then hell, nothing in the entire human involvement was worthwhile.

Let it all fall to hell.

If gentle, harmless people like Valentina Querente and vital young men like Johnny Bolan could not find a safe place to love and prosper in this only world available to them . . . then let it all go to hell.

Midnight could very well become a deadline for death.

He had not been kidding.

Without Johnny and Val at his side, Mack Bolan would never leave Boston. He would die here, and they could bury him here. Along with what was left of Boston. Until midnight, then.

Bolan was not merely posturing before himself.

And he was entertaining no illusions about that meeting with Al 88.

Either way it went, whether the guy actually sprung Johnny and Val or not, Al 88 would have to be desperately determined that Mack the Bastard Bolan would never walk away from Boston Common alive.

Not with what Mack Bolan knew about Albert Greene.

Call it a deadline for death. Until midnight, then. Then somebody was going to die.

Maybe everybody would die at midnight.

Bolan left the decision in the hands of the universe, and he went to find a place to rest his weary bones and to wait out the longest nine hours of his troubled lifetime.

17: The Deployment

It was a few minutes past eight o'clock on the evening of Day Two, when Books Figarone was moving slowly and tiredly as he entered the crumbling warehouse on Boston's waterfront. This had been the most agonizing and exhausting 24 hours the ex-professor had ever lived through, and he was thankful that the thing was coming to a head at last.

The others were waiting for him in the dusty and dimly lighted warehouse office.

Skip Sicilia was there, looking wan and wrung out.

Hoops Tramitelli sat tensely expectant, a nervous tic working at his left eye.

Each had brought a backup man inside with him, and these two were eyeing each other suspiciously from their chairs at the opposite sides of the small office.

Figarone quietly took his place at the table, cleared his throat, and told them, "You understand, I'm here in a double capacity. Let's keep that fact visible. I'm here primarily to present Al 88's recommendations for bringing our thing together again. Secondly, I am here as personal friend and adviser to all principals. Is that understood?"

Tramitelli waved his hand to signify understanding.

"This's no court, right?" Sicilia put into the record.

"It's no court," the *consigliere* assured him. "But we are all bound to the same extent as if it were a court."

"Okay, I go along with that."

Figarone told them, "First we'll take up the internal affairs."

"I'd like to say something first," Tramitelli said quietly. "I think we all got to understand something here. Al 88 is not the enemy. Skip ain't the enemy, and you, counselor, you're not the enemy. Neither am I. Now it's been a hell of a bad time for all of us. We got to keep remembering that we're all together in this. Right? What hurts one of us hurts all of us. Let's bury our hatchets, what ones we might have, right here and now."

Sicilia murmured, "Thanks, Hoops. I'm glad you said that."

Without a word, Figarone produced a small penknife. He pursed his lips and made a small, quick incision in the puffy tip of one of his fingers. Blood oozed onto the table. He passed the knife to Tramitelli and moved his bleeding finger into the center of the table.

Tramitelli duplicated the procedure and passed the knife on to Sicilia who did likewise.

Their blood mingled on the table between them, then they pressed the wounds together and Figarone muttered something in Italian.

The ritual apparently held a deep and emotional significance for all three, even for the educated gentleman from Cambridge. He wrapped a handkerchief around his injured member and smiled at the other two. "Now let's get down to business," he said.

"I apologize for that crummy deal last night, Books," Sicilia murmured. "I guess I lost my head a little."

"It's forgotten."

"Okay. What's this internal affair?"

The lawyer's eyes dwelled on the huge figure of Hoops Tramitelli. "First I think Hoops should know about his inheritance. He gets the territory left behind by the passing of our old friend Manny Greco. That's your country now, Hoops. You get full title to everything Manny had going, and we'll bind all licenses and grants to you without restrictions of any nature."

Tramitelli nodded his head, a sour smile registering briefly upon the tense face. "I hate to get it this way, but I got to say, it's about time. I been playing second and third fiddle for damn near thirty years."

"You're the maestro now," Figarone told him. "Do you have any questions or any representations?"

The veteran triggerman shook his head. "No, it's fine. I'm perfectly satisfied."

"Then accept my congratulations," Figarone said soberly. "I've always respected you, Hoops."

"Thanks."

Figarone then stared at Harold Sicilia for a long moment, then he told him, "You get the territory left vacant by the passing of our old friend Andy Nova, in addition to what's already yours by rights. You get full title to everything Andy had going, and we'll bind all licenses to you in full loyalty and without restrictions of any kind."

Sicilia seemed torn between a smile and a frown. He asked, "What happens to all those other northern territories?"

"For the time being," Figarone replied, "they will be carried under the full protection of Al 88, acting as the representative of *La Commissione*—until such time as final disposition may be made."

"I guess that's okay by me, then," Sicilia replied, pointedly adding, "For now."

The lawyer told him, "I'm not finished with you, Skip. In addition to the foregoing, you get full title to the muscle franchise throughout eastern Massachusetts."

The fisherman's face broke into an ear-to-ear grin. "I guess that's fair enough," he said.

"Well, Al wants everybody to be happy. He wants to cool this area, and get us all pulling together. Uh, in connection with that last, Skip, you'll get the usual tax, assessed according to services performed. You'll answer directly to Al 88 and to nobody else until such time as he is officially relieved of local responsibilities."

"Great. That's great."

"And you'll bind yourself with full loyalty to whomever is eventually recognized as the Boston representative on *La Commissione*."

"Naturally. That goes without having to be said."

"And you pay, within thirty days of this date, a fine of one hundred thousand dollars, as full restitution for the mistake you made here in this present trouble."

The smile slowly faded from the fisherman's broad face. He said, "What's that again now?"

"You heard it, Skip, that's bound into the agreement. The money will be divided among the widows and families left behind by our dear friends who died here during this unfortunate thing that has happened to us. You brought that to us, Skipper, and you will pay the fine."

Sicilia's eyes fell. He lit a cigarette, slowly exhaled a lungful of smoke, and muttered, "Okay, I'll give the money to the survivor's fund."

"That takes care of that, then," the lawyer declared with a sigh of relief. "Now we know where we stand, we can get on to the other business. Where's that merchandise, Skip?"

Sicilia's eyes flickered. He seemed to be trying very hard to keep remembering that the *consigliere* was speaking for Al 88's mouth. He sighed and said, "Not far from here."

"I hope they're in good condition."

"Don't worry about that. I wouldn't let nothing happen to my little golden gooses."

"Fine. We're giving them back to Bolan. At midnight."

Sicilia's eyes wavered, then clashed with Tramitelli's. The troubled gaze returned abruptly to Figarone and he muttered, "I haven't said yet that I want to give them back."

"It's not your decision," the *consigliere* told him. "They are what started all this trouble. They are what is going to end it. The other disposition is tied to this one all the way, Skipper. You can't eat your cake and still keep it."

"It ain't that," Sicilia replied testily. "I just can't stand the thought of giving in to that damn Bolan."

"Who said we're giving in?" Figarone asked, smiling.

"Oh, well, if that—okay then, if you're working something, fine. I'll go along with anything honorable."

"The guy will be at Boston Common at midnight," Figarone said, launching into the explanation without further preamble. "He will be meeting, he thinks, a solid citizen named Greene who will be there as sort of referee. The whole place will be sealed off, there will be a police line surrounding the entire common." He glanced at his watch. "It should have already started. Bolan will think he's walking into a sure thing, no cops or anything, just Greene and the merchandise. He—"

"Just who is this Greene?" Tramitelli asked.

"A do-gooder, big man on the social register. Don't worry, he's harmless. But this is very important. We don't want to get this Greene caught in anything. Al wants that made very clear. We make no move until the do-gooder is clear and free. The guy may come in handy again someday, Al wants him handled with kid gloves."

Figarone was in his own element now and he was relishing the job. He opened his briefcase, withdrew a packet of maps and sketches. "All we have to do," he explained, grinning, "is to get in there and get set up for Bolan. That means we have to get by the cops, going in and going out. They'll probably come a'running at the first sound of gunfire, so make sure you understand the escape route."

Tramitelli was pawing through the sketches. He said, "Somebody has gone to a lot of trouble."

"Right, somebody has," Figarone replied. "This is going to be where Bolan gets his. Al most emphatically states that Bolan has got to get hit. He is not to be allowed out of this one."

"I get his fuckin' head," the fisherman declared. "After what he did to me up at Chelsea, it's my right."

"There probably won't be time for grisly games," Figarone cautioned. "It's going to be nip and tuck, getting out of there before the cops swarm in."

"I'm gonna get his head just the same," Sicilia insisted.

Tramitelli was grinning. He said, "There's a good price on that head. It would take care of your fine and then some. Maybe we should talk about that before we go in. We're going to be in this together. Let's agree on the split right now."

Sicilia shrugged. "Even split, I guess. Okay by me."

The lawyer said, "You'd better kill the guy first. You can divide his head later. Let's get on with this. There's a lot to cover and a lot to be done, and we don't have all night to do it."

Sicilia was smiling serenely, as though reviewing some delicious idea, his eyes cast toward the ceiling.

Tramitelli and Figarone exchanged glances.

Sure, both pair of eyes said. It had all turned up roses for the fisherman from Rockport. The bastard was getting everything he'd set out to get.

Maybe Figarone knew . . . it wasn't ended yet.

It would not be ended until all of them were standing over Mack the Bastard's bleeding body.

Well . . . in less than four hours, they'd all know for sure.

Despite utter exhaustion, Bolan's sleep had been fitful and close to the surface of consciousness. He had dreamed continually, it seemed, and even in his dreams he could not escape the harsh tensions of the Boston situation.

In one vivid encounter with his subconscious, he was battling a dragon with a sword which must have weighed 40 pounds or more. The dragon was holding two "turkeys" in its mouth on a bed of flames. Each time Bolan slashed out at the monster, the sword passed through the body as though there was nothing there but air. He was trying to induce the beast to spit out the "turkeys"—which were headless and had no limbs—and they were flaming. After a seemingly eternal battle, during which he was worn down to stumbling exhaustion, the unruffled dragon ambled away with its flaming turkeys still clasped tightly in its possession and it disappeared into a faraway building which looked suspiciously like the White House in Washington.

He came out of that one threshing and grunting, and he gave it up there and staggered into the bathroom. It was time to be up and away, anyway. It was eight o'clock; he'd been fighting dragons for three hours.

For how long had he been battling the real live ones? With about the same damned results?

Bolan shook away the hopeless feeling and took a quick shower, shocking himself alive with alternating hot and cold water, then he shaved and put on fresh underwear and a black suit that didn't smell of blood and hellfire.

He cracked open a thermos of coffee and consumed all the dry bread and cheese he could stomach, then he got his stuff together and strapped on his weapons.

The Beretta went into the snapout rig beneath his left arm, the AutoMag mini-cannon at his right waist. Into the belt pockets went two extra clips of 9 mm Parabellums for the Beretta and two reloads of the 240-grain magnum heart-stoppers for the fantastic .44.

He clipped on a couple of grenades, just for kickers, then got into the topcoat.

Bolan had long ago given up stopping at hotels and motels; they were much too vulnerable a resting place for the most-wanted man in the country. And so he'd considered himself fortunate to find the South Bay apartment, complete with private garage, on such short notice, even though it left a lot to be desired in terms of comfort and class. All he'd needed, of course, was a safe place to lay his head for a few hours. The old lady who'd rented him the place was about half deaf and it had been obvious that she didn't see too well, either.

So, yeah, it had been a fortunate wind of fate or whatever had blown him this way.

He went out the back way, examined the tamper-seal on the garage door, then he took the battle-scarred vehicle out of there and headed for Back Bay.

He felt renewed, and ready to bring this Boston battle into final focus.

A quick run past the Greene mansion showed all lights blazing but no signs of activity inside or out.

Bolan went on past and parked one block up the street, then he circled back on foot for a more leisurely look.

He was glad he had. Two official vehicles were parked in a narrow alleyway behind the house, a couple of uniformed cops standing between them and quietly passing the time in relaxed conversation.

Something was brewing inside, that was certain.

So, on to the front.

He went back the way he'd come, passing on by his parked vehicle, and proceeded toward the Common on foot.

He sniffed out the police line two blocks below the Public Gardens, a combination of quiet vehicular and foot patrolmen in a rather loose consortment along Clarendon Street.

The purpose of the line was not to keep Bolan out. He understood that. It was to honor the sacred ground which lay just ahead, to keep all others out.

Any thought that Al 88 would play this game straight would be wishful thinking of the most dangerous sort.

It would take more than a line of cops to set Bolan's mind at ease.

Bolan kept his distance and studied the movements of the police for several minutes, then he slipped off his topcoat and discarded it, electing to go the rest of the way in black suit.

The universe was favoring him again tonight. The sky was overcast and the darkness was complete, broken only by regular spacings of street lighting.

He probed along the line until he found the combination he liked, and when he made his move he was no more than a flitting extension of the night.

He worked his way through the gardens and onto the Common; by nine o'clock he had completed a thorough recon of the meeting site and picked out his forward observation post.

He was in good cover and he was comfortable.

His night vision had never been sharper.

He felt mentally alert and ready for whatever might come.

All he had to sweat now was the clock.

This was the one, he supposed, that had been waiting for him all his life.

He had to meet this challenge, and he had to master it. Everything that held meaning to his life was hanging in the balance.

It was not, however, a question of his living or dying; that question was not even to be asked.

It had to do with meaning, the answer to the mystery of life itself.

The only question of this pregnant night would have to be answered by Johnny and Val.

Did the weak and the defenseless always have to fall to the predator? And did it matter, in the final run of things, whether they did or not?

As far as Mack Bolan was concerned, the whole answer would be revealed on Boston Common, in the cradle of liberty, on this night which could end all nights and still all questions for a man called Mack Bolan.

And the Executioner intended to influence the answer to that question with every resource at his command.

He cleared his head, then, of all the excess baggage—of fire-breathing dragons, flaming turkeys and hopeless warriors, put on his combat mind and settled into the long wait.

18: The Answer

At ten o'clock a police cruiser eased into the Common from Park Street and made a slow diagonal crossing, skirting around Frog Pond and creeping on to the junction of Boylston and Charles Streets.

Bolan marked the passage and continued the grim wait.

At ten-thirty a sanitation department truck rumbled onto Charles and invaded the park, making stops at several trash stations. Bolan watched closely and decided that no trash was being picked up . . . but that something was evidently being dropped off.

At each stop, something slid out of the rear of the truck to then disappear into the darkness.

He counted six such debarkations, then the truck went on toward Beacon Hill.

Somebody had slipped some juice to somebody, Bolan was convinced of that. The truck should never have been allowed through the police line.

He kept his eyes and ears alert and began picking them up again as one by one they scurried into positions surrounding the meeting site.

Okay. He had them spotted.

He continued the quiet surveillance for another fifteen minutes and until he had more than their spot—

he had their feel, their smell, he almost had their collective frame of mind.

Here and there the shielded flare of a match or a cigarette lighter, the glow of a cigarette, a cough, nostrils being evacuated—once, even, a soft command passed across the distance.

Yes, these boys were restless, scared, keyed-up, jittery. He knew them all by 11 o'clock—not their names, of course, but what they were—he knew them individually and he knew them collectively and when he had their feel thoroughly absorbed as a subconscious part of himself, the man from jungleland moved softly away from his drop, to begin a maneuver designed to physically cement that growing relationship.

He visited them one by one, and ingested them, quietly, slowly, without fuss or argument; one by one he gathered them into himself in a methodical harvest; one by one he reduced their numbers and thus the combat odds between them. And at 11:30, Bolan was again alone in the cradle of liberty.

At fifteen minutes before the hour of twelve, a man and a woman made an approach from the direction of the Boston Massacre Monument near Tremont Street. They were trudging along stiffly, unhurriedly—moving awkwardly, in a sort of weird single-file.

Bolan watched with interest, catching them once beneath the full glow of an overhead lamp. The man was rather tall, well set up, and handsomely attired in a pearl-gray overcoat with Homburg to match—maybe fifty, maybe less. Bolan had never seen the guy before. The woman, though . . . yes, he had seen that fragile flower, and not too many hours earlier.

Mr. and Mrs. Al 88, Bolan presumed.

He wondered about the woman's presence there,

but not to the point of distraction. The couple passed close beside him and went on to the designated point, just below Frog Pond.

They stood there in the pale glow of a park lamp, hardly moving—not even talking, it seemed.

It was ten minutes before the appointed hour.

Bolan held his position, and at five minutes until twelve another movement came to his alert attention. Someone was moving up from the Boston Common Garage area, it was more than one someone. Several breaths were blending in a hurried pace; several sets of feet were sending out soft telegraphic vibrations along the ground, announcing their approach.

And from up on Beacon Hill, a vehicle engine with an irritating quality was sending its message to the quivering perceptions of the man in black. He knew that sound; he had heard it very recently, very . . .

The someones from the garage area were taking on indistinct visual shapes now. He separated three forms and began analyzing them. And then his heart lurched and he knew that an answer was walking toward him.

Val was there. Johnny was there. And a third vaguely familiar . . . of course, it figured, Books Figarone, every man's *consigliere*.

But those vibrations from Beacon Hill . . .

Bolan made his move then, coming up from his drop in a swift circling of the terrain and closing on the target area with all jungle quietness.

He was poised in the deep darkness twenty feet to the rear of the shark and the goldfish when the threesome downrange again took on identifiable shapes.

Before they could move on into the illumination of the meet site, Bolan's icy tones lofted a command across the Common ground: "Hold it right there, Books!"

The advance became confused, and then halted.

The nervous response came then. "Bolan? It's all right. I have your brother and Miss Querente, right here beside me. Everything's in order."

Point of law, counselor.

Mr. and Mrs. Shark were turned in half-light, staring back into the darkness enveloping the jungle cat at their rear.

"Let me hear them," Bolan called out.

"Yes, Mack, we're all right," sang out the dearly beloved.

"Mack, it's Johnny," the young lion reported in. "This guy says he's the official go-between. Don't trust him. I think he's a weasel."

"Stay put!" tense dragon-slayer commanded. "Not you, Books. You move into the light!"

Al 88 was casting looks in all directions. Wondering where the hell were all the insurance men?

Figarone came on in, moving slowly, jerkily, scared out of his skull. He, also, was showing considerable interest in the surrounding terrain.

"Okay, hold it right there. Look at the guy, Books. Know him?"

"It's supposed to be Mr. Greene," the *consigliere* quavered. "But I never met him, Bolan. Don't blame me if—"

"It's Greene, all right. But he's a man of many names. Tell him who you are besides Guarini, Al."

The guy down there in the lamplight hunched his shoulders and glared morosely into the darkness.

The man from Cambridge was beginning to get the scent. He caught his breath and swayed forward. "Al!" he cried. "Is that . . . ?"

"He's a master of the 88 keys—right, Mrs. Guarini-Greene?"

"Jesus Christ!" Figarone exclaimed.

Not even a reasonable facsimile.

Those vibrations were moving down the hill now, and Bolan was remembering where he'd heard that particular set before.

The frosty voice advised the trusted adviser, "You'd better listen to the man, Books. Listen to him tell you how to handle this situation.

"Guarini! You send the counselor back down the road, you advise him to call off all the headhunters and send them home! Right now, before my thumb tires of restraining this hammer!"

Even Classy Al should know what a dead man's hammer is.

"Do as he says, Books!" urged the suave shark.

"Recognize that voice, Books?"

Figarone jerked halfway about, torn between the light and the darkness. "The truck, Al!" he gurgled.

"Head it off, stop it!" pleaded the man who dined at the White House.

The counselor took off on a desperate mission, flinging himself through the black of night to try to call off a sure thing already set in motion.

Bolan called, "Val, Johnny. Get going, straight ahead! Keep running until you hit a cop!"

The goldfish spoke up for the first time, belaying that order.

"No! Please! Mr. Bolan, let me help. I can get them out of here safely!"

"Why do that?" came the cold response.

"It's why I'm here." The frail woman stepped away from Guarini and held up a tiny revolver for Bolan's distant inspection. "I brought him here with this. I knew what he was planning. Please believe me! There is but one way out!"

Bolan was torn and bleeding inside . . . soul blood.

That sword was beginning to weigh 40 pounds again.

Johnny and Val had not budged. They were awaiting the decision.

Mrs. Shark was still trying. "Why else do you think I would come? I couldn't stand the thought of . . . believe me, there's no way out but one. I brought this pistol to be sure. *Please!*"

She had given the guy an inspiration. Glibly, he made his bid. "She's speaking the truth, Bolan. Believe me, we've *all* got to get out of here now. Let's call a truce and move on while there's still time!"

Bolan advised him, "No way, not for you."

Yeah, okay, not for him. And that meant not for Bolan. But how about the non-combatants? The answer would have to come from them. He called over, "Val? What's your feel?"

"I'll go with her," beloved girl replied immediately. "Can't we all go?"

"I'll be along," Bolan assured her. "I know where you're going. See you there. Now get going! Johnny, take over!"

Mrs. Whoever-the-hell led the way; those two loved ones moved into the light momentarily, both pairs of eyes searching the darkness for a glimpse of the man, then they hurried on behind the lady from Back Bay.

Al 88 was a leaning statue in lamplight, swiveled around off-balance, eyes searching for a differentiation between black and blacker, head tilted, and ears probably cocked for the sound of another kind of hazard.

His voice was sweating as he urged, "Let's get out of here, man."

Bolan replied, "Too late."

And it was.

Headlamps were bouncing across the uneven surface of Common earth, coming up from the lower road, the laboring whining grind of a truck engine in pulling gear telling it like it had to be: a crew wagon to end all crew wagons.

Silhouetted in the glow of the headlamps, a running figure emerged from the darkness downrange, hands over the head and pumping wildly in a crossing motion, trying vainly to stop something that would not be stopped.

A rattle of gunfire split the night, and the running figure of Books Figarone hit the ground flopping, then disappeared beneath the lights.

My debt is paid. You lived past my gun, Books.

Guarini groaned. He took a step toward the darkness and Bolan warned him, "Huh-uh. Stay put!"

"You saw that!"

"You bet I did."

"They'll shoot anything that moves! Those are the orders!"

"Then don't move," Bolan suggested.

The guy hadn't expected to be taken literally, but what he'd meant to imply Bolan already knew.

That was a head party coming across the Boston Common, and they were on safari aboard a sanitation truck. This was fair-game country; anything that was living within these protected grounds, at this dangerous moment, was a candidate for swift death.

The idea was *overkill;* mop up; and if any of the first-wave troops were unlucky enough to still be around at overkill time, then that was one of the misfortunes of war.

The idea was to *get Bolan,* whatever the cost, and to leave him absolutely no way to survive the meet at the Common.

Of course, a fifteen-year-old kid and an entirely harmless young woman would have to bear the misfortune right along with everybody else.

Al 88 must have had a lot of confidence in his timing.

Well, time it now, Al.

"Take off!" Bolan commanded.

The guy did not need much prodding. He hurled himself out of that lamplight like he'd been catapulted, and he actually made about ten flying flings across the Common before his head party caught up to him, and filled his carcass with forty pounds of lead—at least a sword's-full—and ground him into the Boston Common from which he would never, ever, rise again.

Al 88 was a part of the history of the place when Bolan moved out to engage the enemy.

He calculated a point about ten feet to the rear of those moving headlamps and he lobbed a fragmentation grenade into there. The sight and sound of Bolan-at-war split the night with local thunder and lightning, and in the flash bodies could be seen being ejected from the bed of that open truck and floating rather ungracefully to ground. He hit them with the other grenade then, so the hunters already knew that they had become the hunted. The sounds of that discovery came across those historic grounds as a babble of alarm and pain and fear.

Bolan descended upon them then with the minicannon, putting an end to pain and fear.

He poked among the ruins in a final evaluation,

recognized there what was recognizable of Skip Sicilia, Hoops Tramitelli and other outstanding birds of that same feather.

Then he loped off toward the west boundary of the hell-grounds, aware that he would have to evade cops and robbers alike along that freedom path, but confident that the night would carry him through.

Yet the Executioner felt good about the entire experience.

He knew that, in some subtle way, mankind had vindicated itself here tonight, in this cradle of liberty.

The predators did not always have to win.

That answer had arrived, yes—but not, after all, from Johnny and Val.

It had come from a fragile little echo of the blood-lines which had originated this better idea in human relations, about two hundred years ago.

I love my husband, Mr. Bolan. And yet she had . . .

Yeah, the answer had come from a goldfish who had learned to outswim the sharks.

Sure . . . as long as one human being cared that much, then there had to be a valid meaning to the riddle of life. It all fit together, somewhere.

And, yes . . . the Executioner was glad that he'd come to Boston.

EPILOGUE

The kid was just standing there, giving him that awed look—a sort of an embarrassed, shy, don't-know-what-to-say kind of look.

Bolan swept it all away with a joyous whoop, and he lifted the kid brother completely off the floor and swung him around in a bear hug.

When he put him down, tears were flowing unashamedly from every eye in the place, and Johnny had found his voice.

He told the big brother, "That face is hard to take right away, Mack. On a wanted poster, or in a newspaper—that's something else. But to see my brother actually wearing it, well, that's weird."

Bolan asked him, "What's in a face, Johnny?"

The kid had some substance. He didn't even have to think about it . . . or maybe he already had. He just said, "Guess you're right. They're all masks, aren't they?"

And then Johnny very discreetly excused himself to see how Mrs. Greene was doing. "She's pretty well tore up," he explained to a couple who had suddenly found each other with their eyes, and hadn't eyes or mind for anything else at the moment.

Bolan told her, "You look great, Val."

She walked into his arms, and there was not much to be said for the next several minutes.

Then Bolan firmly took her in hand, led her to a chair, gently pushed her into it, and they talked very seriously and at times very emotionally, for the most part of an hour.

When Bolan left the Greene library, Valentina was in tears and he was wearing as grim a face as he had worn all day.

Leopold Turrin, in dark glasses and with a silk muffler draped casually across his chin, met him in the hallway and told him, "Your hour is about up, Sarge—and Trantham is bending the ground rules even for that. I wouldn't waste time shaking this town if I were you."

Bolan grunted, "Yeah." Then he asked his friend, "What does a dead man say to the woman he loves, Leo?"

"God, I don't know," Turrin replied dismally. "But if I ever find out, I'll tell it to Angelina first."

Bolan clasped his shoulder and they walked to the door together. "Put them away again for me, Leo. And tell Johnny . . . well tell him I'm so proud of him I could bust open."

"Okay, sure. Uh, somebody is waiting for you outside."

"Who?"

"Brognola. He wants to talk, but strictly off the record. I don't believe he's had a regular heartbeat since we got that poop on Al 88. He's reading all sorts of things into that bit of intelligence, and I get the feeling that he's scared to even discuss it with his superiors. You know what I mean. These days a guy never knows who he's really talking to."

"Yeah," Bolan said. "I know."

"Well, talk turkey to the guy—oh hell, pardon that expression Talk to him level, and listen to him level, understanding that you're talking to a man, not to a government agency. He's acting purely as an individual right now."

Bolan said, "I understand." He thought he knew what was coming via Harold Brognola.

As a matter of fact, it didn't much matter what the Washington VIP had to say to him Bolan had already decided that Washington would be the next stop on his hellfire trail.

He didn't like the idea of dragons disappearing into his country's hallowed halls . . . not even in dreams.

He opened the door, then gazed back into a mansion which reflected the history of a nation, and he told Leo Turrin, "Tell them I love them Leo."

The undercover cop nodded understandingly. "I'll tell them," he assured the livingest dead man he'd ever known.

And as Turrin watched the man walk away, he remembered another moment just a few impossible mornings ago, when he'd watched the tall warrior stride off into the darkness.

In one of those rare openly philosophical moments, Leo had thought about his own resentments—he had resented being anything other than a human being.

And he had wondered . . . at times such as these, which meant *all* the time for a guy like Bolan . . . what did the Executioner resent the most about *his* situation?

Turrin was feeling philosophical again now, and perhaps for the same reasons as before. He thought about that long bloody trail reaching out from Pittsfield to zig-zag across the country and the world, and he thought about the fantastic kind of man it had to be who had stepped off every mile of that travel. The constant warfare, the unending peril, the eternal vigilance—and there the guy went again, without hardly getting his breath, the Executioner was off on another one.

Yeah, a guy in that situation could logically carry a hell of a large bag of resentment.

But Turrin would never again wonder the question.

He'd seen the answer in those cool blue eyes as the guy wheeled about and went out that door . . . yes, it had come to Leo Turrin in a flash what Mack Bolan resented about his situation.

Nothing.

Yeah, that was the answer or at least it was part of it. The big guy resented none of it. He accepted it, all of it, all of the hell, the anguish, the infinite damned blood . . . and without a whimper. He'd quietly accepted his fate, joined it, made an ally of it. Someday he just might stride away and conquer the whole damn world with it.

Yeah.

The guy probably could do just that.

5-75